W9-BYM-910

NAOMI and ELY'S

NO KISS LIST

a novel

Rachel Cohn *and* David Levithan

Alfred A. Knopf   New York

THIS IS A BORZOI BOOK PUBLISHED BY ALFRED A. KNOPF

KNOPF, BORZOI BOOKS, and the colophon are registered trademarks of Random House, Inc.

www.randomhouse.com/teens

Educators and librarians, for a variety of teaching tools, visit us at
www.randomhouse.com/teachers

Library of Congress Cataloging-in-Publication Data
Cohn, Rachel.
Naomi and Ely's no kiss list / by Rachel Cohn and David Levithan. — 1st ed.
p. cm.
SUMMARY: Although they have been friends and neighbors all their lives, straight Naomi and gay Ely find their relationship severely strained during their freshman year at New York University.
ISBN 978-0-375-84440-9 (trade) — ISBN 978-0-375-94440-6 (lib. bdg.)
[1. Interpersonal relations—Fiction. 2. Homosexuality—Fiction. 3. Dating (Social customs)—Fiction. 4. New York (N.Y.)—Fiction.] I. Levithan, David. II. Title.
PZ7.C6665Nao 2007
[Fic]—dc22
2006039727

Printed in the United States of America
August 2007
10 9 8 7 6 5 4 3 2 1
First Edition

To Nancy the First

Thanks to our friends, family, and teen author crew, as always. For this book, specific thanks to Anna, Martha, Nick, Patty, Robin, all the kind folks at Knopf (with a special shoutout to Nancy, Allison, and Noreen), and the fine people at William Morris (particularly Alicia and Jennifer). And thank you to the fans who write to us; you always make our day.

SHIVER

I lie all the time.

I lied to Mrs. Loy from the fourteenth floor when I assured her that I walked her dog three times a day and watered her plants while she went to Atlantic City to win the money for her son's sad operation (or for her own elective plastic surgery—I'm not sure).

I lied to the co-op board of my family's apartment building about my mom's episode that left our living room wall in partial collapse soon after Dad left. I also backed up Mom's lies to the board that we'd pay for the damage. Monkeys will fly outta my butt before we'll be able to come up with the money to fix the fallout. The way I figure, if Mom and I aren't bothered by living in ruins, why should the co-op board care?

I lied to the NYU Admissions Committee that I care about my future and my education. I'm barely a year out of high school, and already I know this NYU deal is a losing proposition. I live out the college freshman lie to hold on to the only thing in my life that's not in ruins—Ely.

I lied to Robin (♀) from psych class when I assured her

that Robin (♂) from that time at the Starbucks at Eighth and University ♥ her and will call her. There's no $$$ for me to move into the school dorms, and Robin's a sophomore with a rare single who goes home on the weekends and lets me use her place when I need to escape The Building. The apartment building where I've lived my whole life may be situated on prime Greenwich Village real estate, but escape from it is my prime priority: escape from parent drama or my lies or Mr. McAllister, the creepy up-and-down elevator man who lives down the hall from Mrs. Loy and who's been ogling me since I was thirteen and my breasts first announced themselves in the elevator mirror.

I've lied to Mom every time I've told her I've stayed the night at Robin's when really I've stayed over at my boyfriend's dorm room. I lie to myself that I need to lie about my whereabouts. It's not like Bruce the Second and I are doing it. We're more about a 📖 in bed, then turn out the light, and ☺—just sleep—'til he leaves in the morning for his 🕐 accounting class. I lie to him that I think accounting is a worthwhile subject to study.

I lied to Robin (♂) when he won our chess game in Washington Square Park after that time with Robin (♀), and the price of my loss was my supposed obligation to answer Truth to his midnight question. Robin said he'd watched five men trip over themselves from checking me out, while I merely glared at them. Robin wanted to know if I use my beauty for good or evil. Evil, I assured him. Lie. Truth: I'm as pure as

2

fresh snow over Washington Square Park on a winter morning, before the dogs and people and machines of this hard, hard city batter its perfect, peaceful beauty.

I lied to Bruce the Second when I promised we would have sex, the real kind, soon. Very soon. We'd barely made it to ♋ when his R.A. walked in and interrupted us. It felt like cheating on Ely.

I lied to Bruce the First when I let him believe he would be my first. Ely is supposed to be first. I can wait. Then maybe I'll let Bruce the Second truly be second.

I lied to the three different men and one girl at the Astor Place Starbucks who eyed me in the wall mirror today and then wanted to sit in the empty chair opposite mine. I pretended I didn't hear them through my 🎧. They could go ⓟ themselves elsewhere. I placed my feet up on the empty chair, to reserve it for Ely. Only Ely.

Mostly, I lie to Ely. 👁 lie to ee-lie.

Ely calls my cell while I lie in wait for him. "I'm running late. Be there in about fifteen minutes. Hold my chair for me. Love you." He hangs up before I can reply. I lie to Starbucks that I even drink Starbucks while lounging around in their chairs, killing time.

We've already survived so much together, what's fifteen minutes more to wait for him? His absence is time gained to spool my un-truths.

I lied to Ely when I told him I forgive his mom for what happened between our parents. I lied to Ely that I'm happy for him since his parents worked things out and stayed together even though mine didn't and now my dad lives not in The Building anymore, far away.

I lied to my mom that the damage is done but it's fine if she needs to take her time to process the fallout before she can find her future. I lied by comforting her that I believe she'll make it through. It's not that I don't think she can. She just doesn't want to.

I lie to all the related parties when I let them believe Dad calls my cell to check in on me every week. Once a month (the odd-numbered ones) is more like it.

Dad's not worried about me. He knows I have Ely.

Ely rarely leaves me, or ends a phone call, without first telling me "I love you." It's Ely's way of saying "good-bye"— like a promise toward our future time together. I lie when I throw back the words "I love you, too."

The complexity embedded in the different levels of meaning that go along with the words "I love you" ought to be a whole mindfuck of a video game, if anyone ever wanted to develop the concept.

Player One: Naomi.

Level 1: "I love you" to my mom, meaning I love you for giving me life, nurturing me, driving me crazy but still inspiring me, even through your heartache. Basic.

Level 2: "I love you" to my dad, said with sincerity that's tinged with coldness, distrustful whether he can actually deliver on the sentiment when he returns it. Harder.

Level 3: The playful "I love you" I throw at my boyfriend

when he waits for me outside my class with a hot coffee and a donut. This grade of "I love you" is understood to have no intent whatsoever of L-O-V-E *luuuv*. Our relationship is too new for that, and he understands this, too. When Bruce the Second says "I love you" after I . . . do certain things with him, he is careful to immediately divert away, like "I love you when you yell at the frat guys making too much noise down the halls when we're alone in my room. You give most excellent bitch tirade, and now all those guys only envy me more. I love you for that." Whatever.

Levels 4–9: Expressions of passion for the great loves of my life, like disco music, Snickers bars, the Cloisters, the NBA, stairwell games, the luck to have a life lived with Ely.

Here's where the game gets trickiest.

Level 10 (but on a whole other plane, where maybe numbers can't even exist): When I tell Ely "I love you," but I'm *not* lying to him. I'm lying to myself. He absorbs my words as if they're natural, coming from his best friend / almost-a-sister. And Player One: Naomi *does* mean it that way. Genuinely. But maybe other ways, too. The confusing and impossible ways.

Game stalled.

Truth intrudes.

Lies are easier to process.

I lied to Ely that I'm okay with gay. I am. Just not for Ely. He was supposed to belong to me in the Happily Ever After. Manifest destiny.

I lied to Ely that of course I recognized *his* true manifest destiny was the queendom of queerdom and hadn't that been obvious all along? *Right! And great! Except not!* We've practically been promised to each other from childhood, grew up side by side, his family in 15J, mine in 15K. Naomi & Ely. Ely & Naomi. Never one without the other. Just ask anyone within a ten-block radius of the Fourteenth Street Whole Foods, where the entire Indian hot-bar section witnessed the disaster fallout between our two sets of parents. Naomi & Ely: played doctor (♂) / nurse (♀) together; learned how to kiss while rehearsing in private for the lead roles in our junior high production of *Guys and Dolls* together; shared a locker and their high school experiences together; and chose to attend NYU together, chose to remain side by side at home instead of move into the nearby dorms, for reasons of cost efficiency and of Naomi & Ely co-dependency.

When Ely finally finds me at Starbucks, he's breathless and red-cheeked from running in the winter cold. He collapses into the chair I've reserved for him.

I hand Ely the hot chocolate the Starbucks manager comped me. "Get up," I tell him. "We gotta go."

"Why, Naomi?" he pleads. "Why? I only just got here."

I grab his free hand and we're off, right back outside onto the cold, hard pavement, where we immediately fall into the typical Naomi & Ely routine of hand-and-cup-holding, hurried-walking-and-talking-while-maneuvering-through-sidewalk-people lockstep.

"Trust me," I say.

He doesn't ask where I'm leading him. "Was it so necessary to make me miss the MacDougal Street café study session with the cute T.A. from my econ class to discuss your latest misdiagnosis? You don't have cancer, Naomi. And in case you didn't notice, it's like thirty degrees outside and there are ways I'd rather be spending my time than freezing my ass off walking down this sidewalk. For instance, making eyes at the cute T.A.—in a heated café, by the way." Ely extracts his one hand from mine, gives his hot chocolate over to me to hold with his other hand, and then places both his hands together at his mouth, to warm them. I want to do the breathing for him.

It would not be a lie to say I like cold. It's what I yearn for most. To shiver.

"How can you not be concerned that I might have cancer?" I ask. "I found a lump on my breast." *Touch it, Ely. Touch it.*

"Lie. Not only are you biting your lip, which you always do when you lie, but your mom told me about the alleged lump in the elevator this morning. The doctor said it was an overgrown pimple."

Monkeys!

I must distract Ely from my lie. I stop us at a fence in front of a schoolyard playground. The school building behind it is massive, dank and dirty, graffiti-covered, with bars on the windows. The playground is all blacktop surrounded by dilapidated fence grating.

"I think we should get married here," I tell Ely.

"Oh, my darling Naomi, you're making me swoon from the gritty romance of it all. What happened to the Temple of

Dendur inside the Met? I agreed to that one just so I can see you wearing the Nefertiti ivory gown, with Cleopatra kohl-eyes. You're one girl who could totally pull off the ancient Egyptian goddess look."

"What will the groom wear?"

"The same."

✗ ✗ ✗

Wrong wrong wrong.

I must correct him.

"Not *you* and me get married here, Ely. Me and *he*." I point to the hoops player on the blacktop who's just landed an amazing three-pointer in the netless basketball rim. The player reaches his arms up and out in a V pose, causing the hoodie over his head to fall to his shoulders and present his beautiful face for our full viewing pleasure.

Ely's eyes meet mine. "So worth missing a study session for," he says, smiling.

He should know to trust me. Even when I'm lying.

We admire. Gabriel is not only the hottest guy on the court, he's also the star player. Run. Pass. Jump. Dunk. WOW. Graveyard-shift doorman by night, superstar pickup b-ball player by day.

When the game ends, the players leave the court, sprinting off toward warm homes, I hope. Ely and I duck our heads low as they pass our salivating-at-the-fence, *la-di-da,* nothing-to-notice-here stance.

Once they're gone, Ely bows down to me, as I'm owed.

Discovering the early-evening hangout place of the new night doorman at our building, whom everyone in our building wants to know more about—but no one really knows anything about him other than how gorgeous he is, and whatever more there is to know, Gabriel's not telling—that's some prime sleuthing on my part.

When he raises himself from his bow, Ely turns around and slumps his back against the fence. He lets out an infatuated sigh. "I can't believe we haven't done this earlier, but clearly Gabriel belongs on the No Kiss List. Let's put him at the bottom, since he's new. He should work his way up."

Ely and I created the No Kiss List™ in the aftermath of a long-ago Spin the Bottle party, still sometimes referred to as the You-Made-Out-With-Me-To-Make-Donnie-Weisberg-Jealous! 👽! Incident. Our No Kiss List™ is an ever-changing one, almost like a sentient being, chemically formed by Ely's ratio of Obsessive Study Time vs. Observational Boy Crush Time, and my ratio of PMS vs. boredom. By agreeing in advance that certain people are off-limits, even truly, madly kissable ones—I'm talking it *hurts* knowing that person's lips will never touch yours because of your own vow of no-kissiness—Ely and I keep our friendship free of jealousy. The No Kiss List™ is our insurance against a Naomi & Ely breakup.

If our parents had created a No Kiss List™, they could have saved us all a lot of grief. The next generation won't make that mistake.

I tell Ely, "Okay to adding Gabriel to this list, but I

disagree about his standing. Gabriel's hotter than anybody on there now. I vote for him to go directly into number two position."

"Deal," Ely says.

Interesting. That concession was most easily won.

Bookies, take note. Updated top standings on the No Kiss List™:

#1: Donnie Weisberg, still—the grand symbol over whom we vow to remain chaste, to protect the sanctity of the institution that is Naomi & Ely. The fact that we have no idea where Donnie is these days—we've heard rumors he's doing some Habitat for Humanity shit in Guatemala to dodge a drug rap after that senior skip-day 'shroom party last spring—has no relevance to Donnie's permanent #1 standing on the No Kiss List™;

#2: Welcome, Gabriel, hot midnight doorman, lusted after by every Building resident with a pulse, except maybe creepy Mr. McAllister, who apparently needs at least C-cup cleavage action to get off;

#3: My cousin Alexander (Kansas All-State tight end— 'nuff said);

#4: Ely's cousin Alexandra (East Village, standing ovation for her performance in the experimental stage version of *The Crying Game*—'nuff said);

#5: Robin (♂), cuz both Ely and I like Robin (♀), who really likes Robin (♂), and Robin (♀) is my symbol proving that I can make friends in college outside of Naomi & Ely; and

#6: The tweedy theology grad student guy who is illegally subletting apartment 15B.

"How'd you know Gabriel plays basketball here?" Ely asks.

"Happened to walk by this playground one day and noticed him here," I say.

The itsy-bitsy 🕷 crawls up the lying wall.

I've never, ever kissed Gabriel. I've never, ever had more than a five-minute conversation with Gabriel without Ely present.

But.

I *may* have exchanged digits with Gabriel. He *may* occasionally text me. He *might* have mentioned where he sometimes plays ball with his boys before his night shift starts.

"Lucky break for us!" Ely says.

Installing Gabriel directly at #2 will keep the Naomi & Ely ☻ safe. Otherwise, down *may* come the ☂ and wash Naomi out.

"Reminder," I say. "How much do I love you to give up ever having a chance with a Gabriel?"

"Reminder. You have a boyfriend already."

I do need the reminder. "You're right. Bruce Two is waiting for me. I gotta go."

My boyfriend and I have our own study session planned: He studies while I avoid studying. I like to iron Bruce's shirts while he studies at his desk, occasionally looking up from his laptop or his textbooks to smile at me in his boring but pleasing kind of way. Great teeth. Bruce will say, "Naomi, I wear plain black T-shirts from the Gap. They really don't need ironing." And I'll say, "So?" Because ironing for him is somewhat more fun than making out with him. It's, like, orderly, and reasonably fine time suckage. The ironing, and the kissing. And when the mandated interval of Bruce's five-minute study-break time beeps from his cell phone alarm clock, he'll stand up and cuddle me from behind, nestling his head into the curve between my neck and shoulder. Probably not developing a woody while pressed against me because that would interfere with his study schedule. But he will whisper into my ear, "God, you're pretty." Like he's so proud of that. Like I had anything to do with a set of fucked-up genes delivering me shiny hair, a pleasant enough face, and a desirable body I don't really put to use.

Let's be honest. Even counting the No Kiss List™ members stricken from my lair, this body does not lack for attention, if I want it. But I should wait for Ely to inaugurate it. I owe him that. We've been planning our wedding since we were twelve, when Ely proposed as a means to extract from me the first real kiss we shared, together. *Gay* doesn't change that—our shared past, our committed future. *Gay* doesn't mean I shouldn't wait for that one moment when he won't be.

I reach for Ely's hand. Game over. Time for us to leave.

But Ely stays rooted on the sidewalk, slumped against the fence.

Wait a minute. *Shazam* 🗯 *alacazam!* as Ely and I used to scream in the building elevator before lighting up all the floors to annoy Mr. McAllister. Ely gave in too easily—to vaulting Gabriel to #2 on the No Kiss List™ and to enabling my class-skipping habit by showing up when he had a study session. Ely busts his ass maintaining a high GPA to keep his freshman scholarship in good standing. He's got to. His parents make too much money for them to qualify for need-based financial aid but not enough to pay the full tuition tab and their mortgage. Ely is trapped by that scholarship as much as my mother and I are trapped in the apartment across the hall from his. Mom's administrative job at the university may cover the tuition for my general studies program, but she could never finance us moving from The Building, no matter how awkward the situation might be with the neighbors. Mom could never afford on her own a place as nice as the one her parents bought for us.

"What's wrong?" I ask Ely. His face has warmed up a little, and without the shiver-flush reddening his cheeks, I can see the worry lines around his beautiful blue Ely-eyes.

"I have to tell you something."

"What?" I ask, concerned. What if Ely has cancer, or he's decided to take out a student loan to move into student housing and out of The Building; or maybe he's so mad about my lies he's no longer going to care if I skip school and fail out entirely.

Ely says, "I kissed Bruce the Second."

DIAL

There are all kinds of ways to force yourself to decide. We do it all the time, make decisions. If we actually thought about every decision we made, we'd be paralyzed. Which word to say next. Which way to turn. What to look at. Which number to dial. You have to decide which decisions you're actually going to make, and then you have to let the rest of them go. It's the places where you think you have a choice that can really mess you up.

She wasn't home. That's the first factor. The doorman let me up, I rang the bell, and she wasn't there, where she said she would be. Two months ago this would have surprised me, but now it just annoyed me. You know that feeling of waiting for someone. I mean *really* waiting for someone—standing in front of a restaurant in the cold and having hundreds of people pass you on the sidewalk. And you don't want to do anything else, because you're afraid you might miss something—that somehow if you don't spot her right away, she'll walk right by. So you stand there and you don't do anything except think about how you're standing there.

Occasionally you might look at your watch, or check your cell phone to see if it's accidentally on silent, even though you already checked for that a minute ago.

That's what dating Naomi was starting to feel like.

I called her and hung up when it answered without ringing, because what good would it be to leave a third voice mail message? What good is it *ever* to leave a third voice mail message?

I was just standing there, trying to figure out how long I should wait. Then Ely's door opened and he came out in his bare feet, carrying a garbage bag to the chute. He took one look at me, smiled, and said, "Let me guess."

We'd never really made it past *comes with the territory* territory. He wasn't really into me, because he thought I was boring, and I wasn't really into him, because he thought I was boring. But when Naomi wanted us to hang out together, we were fine. I got to be the innocent bystander. I wasn't jealous of him—how could I be, when he was gay? No, I was jealous of *them*—the way it was like they had grown up watching all the same TV shows, only the TV show they always kept referring to was their own life together, and each episode was funnier than the last. Every now and then, Naomi (and even Ely) would make the effort to explain one of their references to me, but the act of explaining made it even more awkward, even more obvious. My only comfort was that eventually the night would end and Naomi would go home with me, not him. I knew Ely didn't think I was worthy, but I had a feeling he'd never think anyone was worthy of Naomi. Just like she'd never be happy if he was with anyone else. In old-movie terms, you had to think of it like this: Fred Astaire had a wife who wasn't Ginger Rogers, and Ginger Rogers had a husband (actually, a few of them, I think) who wasn't Fred Astaire. But was there ever any doubt who their true dance partners were? I could be Naomi's boyfriend, sure. I could be the one she slept with (or didn't). But I was pretty certain I'd never be her dance partner.

Ely asked me if I wanted to come inside, and I figured why not. I mean, I figured this would give me a reason to leave a third message, and would give Naomi a place to find me when she showed up. It was much better than waiting in the hallway.

No one else was home. I was curious to meet his parents; Naomi had alluded to them enough for me to put the story together. I know it's wrong, but I always pictured his mother, the one Naomi's father had the affair with, to be attractive. It made more sense that way, at least to me. And Ely was attractive, too. It's not like I didn't know that, although I really didn't think it meant anything to me. It wasn't like I *felt* it, the way I felt it when there was a hot girl around. Like Naomi, who was not only hot but actually happened to like having thoughts. I'd found, in my very limited dating and only-slightly-less-limited friendship experience, that there were a lot of people who treated thoughts like they were a nuisance. They weren't intrigued by them. They didn't go out of their way to prolong them. But Naomi valued the fine art of thinking. The only hitch was that I didn't know what she was thinking. I imagined Ely would have a better idea.

We went into one of those rooms that's lined floor-to-ceiling with bookcases, where the books have been sitting on the shelves together for so long that they look like they've merged into one multi-spined line.

"Can I take your coat?" Ely asked. I handed it over and he threw it on a chair. Which should have been obnoxious, but the way he did it—like he was laughing at himself more than me—made it almost charming. I sat down on the couch and he hovered in front of me.

"Can I offer you a drink?"

It would make more sense, perhaps, if I'd decided yes. But I said no.

He said, "Good. Brandy can get you in trouble, I hear."

"Who's Brandy?" I asked.

"My mother's brandy," he said.

I was confused. "I didn't think you had a mom named Brandy," I said.

Now *he* looked confused. "I don't."

"But you just said she's Brandy?"

He laughed. "She's more ginny than that."

"She goes by Ginny?"

"You have to stop," he said, really laughing. "You're killing me."

I laughed now, too, still confused. "But who's Brandy?" I asked.

"I told you—MY MOTHER'S!"

At this point, he was absolutely cracking up, and I found myself laughing right beside him. He was turning bright red, which made me laugh even harder. Anytime it started to subside, he would yell "WHO'S BRANDY?!?" and I would yell "YOUR MOTHER!" and we would break back down into eye-tearing, bladder-threatening snorts and whinnies. I was keeled over, wiping my eyes. He sat down on the couch next to me and laughed and laughed and laughed.

You have to understand: I don't laugh often. Not out of choice. I just don't get the opportunity. So when I do, it's a dam bursting. It's something opening.

"Knock knock!" I said.

"Who's there?" he asked.

"Orange!" I said.

"Orange who?" he asked.

"ORANGE YOU GLAD TO SEE ME!" I screamed.

It was the funniest thing either of us had ever heard.

"What did the mayonnaise say to the refrigerator?" he yelled to me.

"YOUR MOTHER!" I yelled back.

"Close the door, I'm dressing!"

We went on like this for at least twenty minutes. Every joke we'd ever heard in third grade was dredged up for a command performance. And if we met a pause, we just yelled "ORANGE!" or "YOUR MOTHER!" until the next joke came.

Finally we needed to catch our breath. We were still on the couch. He was leaning into me. I looked at his bare feet and decided to take off my shoes. As I did, he said, "The other shoe drops."

And I said, "No—that was just the first."

He looked at me and it honestly felt like the first time he'd ever seen me.

"I like you," he said.

"Try not to sound so surprised," I found myself replying.

He leaned his head so far back that he was looking at me upside down. I actually thought, *He's even attractive upside down.* And I couldn't even feel attractive right-side up.

"It doesn't matter if I'm surprised or not," he told me. "It matters that I like you."

We heard the elevator stop outside. Gingerly, Ely jumped up and looked through the peephole of his front door. I took off my other shoe.

"Just Mr. McAllister," he said. "Don't worry."

I understood the "Don't worry." Because I'll admit: I didn't want it to be Naomi in the elevator. I wanted to stay like this. I wasn't just enjoying Ely's company; I was enjoying my own as well.

"Let's listen to music," Ely said.

I said sure, assuming he'd turn on the stereo in the living room. But instead he led me to his room, which was covered with poems he'd xeroxed and photographs of his friends, Naomi especially. He scanned his computer for the album he wanted, then pressed play. I recognized it immediately—Tori Amos, *From the Choirgirl Hotel.* It seemed to loosen itself from the speakers as it fell into the room. I thought Ely would sit in a chair or lie on the bed, but instead he lowered himself down on the hardwood floor, facing the ceiling as if it was a sky. He didn't tell me what to do, but I lowered myself next to him, felt the floor beneath my back, felt my breathing, felt . . . happy.

Song followed song. At one point, I realized I'd left my phone in my jacket, which meant I wouldn't hear it if it rang. I let it go.

There was something about our silence that made me feel comfortable. He wasn't talking to me, but I didn't feel ignored. I felt we were part of the same moment, and it didn't need to be defined.

Finally I said, "Do you think I'm boring?"

He turned his head to me, but I kept looking up.

"Why do you say that?" he asked.

"I don't know," I mumbled, a little embarrassed that I'd said anything.

I thought he'd turn back to the ceiling, to the music. But instead he looked at me for almost a minute. Eventually I turned on my side so I could look right back at him.

"No," he finally said. "I don't think you're boring. I do think there are times you don't allow yourself to be interesting . . . but clearly that can change."

How can you spend hours every day trying in small ways to figure out who you are, then have a near-stranger give you a sentence of yourself that says it better than you ever could?

We lay there looking at each other. It made both of us smile.

Then, out of the blue—the blue deep within me—I found myself saying, "I like you, too. Really. I like you."

There is something so intimate about saying the truth out loud. There is something so intimate about hearing the truth said. There is something so intimate about sharing the truth, even if you're not entirely sure what it means.

And that's when he leaned in and kissed me once, lightly, on the lips. As if he'd read exactly what I needed.

It broke the spell. It's not that I stopped being happy. I was still inexplicably, utterly happy. But suddenly the happiness had implications.

My face must have shown it.

"I shouldn't have done that," Ely said, his voice freaking out a little.

"No," I told him.

"Really, I shouldn't have."

He sat up, and I lay there a few seconds more, staring at the space he'd just left. Then I sat up, too. And stood up. And found myself leaving, without actually deciding to leave.

He stayed where he was, but turned to face me when I got to the doorway. I made noises that sounded like excuses for leaving, and he made noises that sounded like understanding why I had to leave.

But before I could go, he said, simply, "I wanted to."

And I waited until I had decided to really leave before I told him, "I did, too."

Then I was gone—out his door, putting my shoes on, grabbing my jacket, then out the front door, past her front door, down the elevator, out of the building, deciding to cross streets, deciding to wait for lights, deciding to put my hands in my pockets. Deciding that none of these things mattered. None of these things involved who I was, only what I did.

The whole night, the whole morning, the whole afternoon now . . . I miss Ely, and I miss Naomi. I miss how much easier life was just twenty-four hours ago.

I think about him a lot.

I think about her a lot.

But I think about him more.

"Really. I like you."

I decide to take out my phone for the first time since I scared myself away from him. I decide not to check the three new messages. I decide to make a call. To start to wrestle with the implications. To maybe get back closer to the happiness.

I just have to decide who to call.

INSOMNIA

I've tried everything. Ambien, Lunesta, melatonin, counting sheep, The Best of Johnny Carson: The 1970s, Charlie Rose: The Present, Charlie Daniels, MTV2, 976-SLUTS4U, the complete works of Dostoyevsky, the complete works of Nicholas Sparks, completely jacking off, Jack Daniel's, the Jackie Chan oeuvre. But nothing and no one can get me to sleep at night.

Blame Naomi.

She was seven. I was five. Our mommies had hustled us into the elevator, but in their two-second pause in the hallway to exchange mismatched mail, the elevator door closed and Naomi and I were left unattended. The elevator went up. Naomi said, "Would you like to see my underwear?" I nodded. She lifted her dress to her stomach. She wore the same kind of pink hipster briefs with elastic lace around the waist that my twin sister, Kelly, wore, but on Naomi, the hipster briefs looked entirely different. Bewitching instead of stupid. I can still recall that exact moment when Naomi dropped her dress back down to her knees and stuck her tongue out at me.

Because my heart? It actually leaped, and hasn't returned to me since. Naomi owned it forevermore.

Flash forward ten years to last spring, Naomi and I in the elevator at the same time again, only this time we're taller, curvier (her), hairier (me). It's not like we didn't see each other regularly at school and in the building, but somehow, for reasons the universe has never bothered to explain to me, this time was different. Naomi appraised me head to toe as the elevator went up. She announced, "You've filled out nicely, freshperson." "I'm a sophomore," I corrected her, grateful my squeaky-voice stage had long passed. "Even better," she said. "Come here, sophomore." I ventured closer to her. She smelled like baby powder and pretty girl shampoo. She leaned into me, her head slanted, her mouth opened ever so slightly. I thought, *No, the wet dream of what I think is about to happen could not actually be about to happen.* I mean, it's not like I'd never kissed a girl before. How many Spin the Bottle parties had I thrown just trying to make such contact with Naomi, anyway? If only I'd known all I needed to do was trap myself in an elevator and wait for Naomi. Then, contact. It happened. Naomi kissed me—slowly, on the mouth, sucking my soul into hers, floors four through fourteen. She tasted like she'd just eaten a Snickers bar. I love Snickers.

I know I know I know. I shouldn't love a girl who toys so casually with other people's feelings, specifically mine, but it's not like my mind has the ability to overrule my heart—and the other parts of my anatomy. See, what people (and by *people,* I mean my sister, our friends, and most of the MySpace community) don't understand about Naomi—except maybe Ely, he gets her, but I hate him, so his understanding doesn't count—is that there's more to Naomi than just the obvious evil. They don't know how she tests out gummy bears for me, pressing them between the plastic cover to find the ones that are freshest, the way I like. They don't know that despite her brazen kisses, her symbols and her lies, her obsession with visiting and chronicling every Starbucks in the universe (though she never orders a single drink; she just plops down in the big purple chair and waits for some guy or girl to fall in love with her), Naomi's really a nice, simple girl at heart. *I* know this about her. *I* know that for all her boasting, ♋ to her means with your clothes still on, talking about movies and life and dreams, tickling toes. *I* know that I am and shall forevermore be Bruce the First to her—in every way. Bruce the Second—I laugh at you! One, two . . . a *million* lifetimes lived without her since Naomi took up with Bruce the Second, but I remain confident that he who shall have the last laugh will be Bruce the First. HAH!

The problem, says my sister, Kelly, is not that I can't get over Naomi—it's that I refuse to. You are correct, sir! Loving Naomi and waiting for her to come back to me—it's not a stalker thing, but more like a personal mission. A job. Wake up, think about Naomi. Go to school, think about Naomi. Come home, eat dinner, do homework, think about Naomi. A few games of Xbox, a few IMs with whoever's available while thinking about Naomi (except for Ely—blocked! blocked! blocked!), download some porn that looks like Naomi, try to

25

go to sleep. Count Naomi sheep. Fail to fall asleep. Naomi Naomi Naomi.

When insomnia prevails and I don't have Naomi physically present to comfort me through it—although in every other way, believe me, she's there—I know I can count on an emergency meeting of the Bruce Society to get me through the night. In the spacious lobby of our one hundred–unit apartment building, the Bruces Below Fourteenth Street convene to pass the dark hours. Sleepless? Big deal. We've got important issues to discuss—specifically, the Burden of Being a Bruce.

We are:

- Mr. McAllister, who alleges to be named Bruce, but I don't imagine anyone would ever dare address him by a name other than Mr. McAllister.
- Gabriel the graveyard-shift doorman, middle name Bruce (fact-checked on driver's license).
- One of Ely's moms, Sue, who may or may not have once been married to someone named Bruce. The University Place Stitch 'n' Bitch knitting circle is hot with rumor over that one.
- Random persons hanging out in the lobby between late-night laundry loads, Bruces in spirit.
- Bruce the Chihuahua, also known as "Cutie Pie" by her owner, Mrs. Loy, but renamed by the Bruces-in-spirit because I'm the one, not Naomi, who feeds and walks her when Mrs. Loy goes out of town. I'm the "nice boy" (take that, Naomi's sainted Ely) who

uses the secret key under Mrs. Loy's mat to tap on Mrs. Loy's apartment door for the dog to hear, but not so loud as to wake Mrs. Loy, when Cutie Pie–sometimes–called–Bruce yelps for a midnight walk.

The problem with the Bruce Society is that I want to talk about being a Bruce, but the other Bruces, they want to talk about insomnia. What insomniacs don't realize is that the more you talk about your inability to sleep, the more you will be unable to sleep. It's like a whole mathematical problem that equals up to a solution called: Why Not Just Face It, You're Screwed. The other members—I question their dedication to the Bruce Society. I suspect they care more about their sleepless nights than about what it means to be a Bruce. Because think about it. There's the legacy of great Bruces whom we should honor and hope to emulate: Lenny the brilliant comedian; Mr. Springsteen; Master Lee; Robert the Bruce, aka "Braveheart." But there are also those Bruces whom we need to seriously consider repudiating, and striking from our namesake society: Willis, Jenner, Hornsby.

Sue/Bruce never fails to dodge the importance of being Bruceness. Instead she asks me, "Honey, have you talked with a shrink about the sleeping issue? I'm worried you look awful tired. You're too young to be an insomniac. Don't you have SATs coming up? You need to get this sleeping issue resolved before then."

I don't know why I like Sue so much. Maybe because she's

not the DNA part of the Ely equation (I don't think), or maybe because she's not part of the Naomi & Ely parental situation that got the co-op board into such a state. I mean, it's one thing to turn fifty and all of a sudden cross over into being midlife-crisis "flexibly" gay; it's an entirely different matter to mess with your neighbor's real estate standing. The consensus from the Bruce Society, in those middle-of-the-night insomniac gossip sessions when Sue isn't present, is that if Ginny had needed to "experiment" so badly, it would have been helpful for the fifteenth-floor residents of our building if she had chosen a man who lives in, like, a different building entirely. And, a man more discreet than Naomi's dad. We'd totally pass a resolution in support of Sue if ever called upon by the co-op board.

Since she doesn't seem to have a clue, I tell Sue/Bruce, "I like not sleeping. Sleeping is time not spent living."

Mr. McAllister the Bruce says, "Sixteen is an age not worth living. Too stupid to know any better. I read in *Marie Claire* that sleep apnea is linked to . . ."

Proof! Naomi swears Mr. McAllister steals her mother's fashion magazines from the garbage-chute-room recycle bin. According to Naomi, the models in those magazines are like porn for old guys too cheap to buy an Internet connection to get it like the rest of us.

Sue / Bruce ignores Mr. McAllister / Bruce like she always does. She pats my shoulder. "Have you given more thought to where you'd like to go to college? Last time we discussed it, you were hung up on colleges that have presidents with Bruce in their names. I'm hoping I was successful in talking you out of that idea?"

She's so nice, Sue/Bruce. "You were. I have a new college plan, as of today. This morning I saw an ad on the subway for a college called PolyTechnic University. According to their slogan, it's a university for people who aren't *mono*-thinkers, but who are *poly*-thinkers. Must mean it's the college for me."

"That's what you are—a poly-thinker?"

"Yes," I state.

What else could I be? If I were a mono-thinker, I probably wouldn't be an insomniac. How is a poly-thinker supposed to fall asleep, and more importantly, *stay* asleep, when thoughts just won't stop darting! darting! darting! through my head?

Lights out. *What is Naomi doing this very minute? Is she naked?*

Tucked in. *Has Bruce the Second seen her naked?*

Fluff pillow. *I've seen Naomi naked.*

Mono-hand maneuver. Jesus Christ. Why bother with porn?

Discard Kleenex under bed. *True, she kept her panties on. And I wasn't allowed to touch. But I've SEEN.*

Toss. Turn. Torture.

A poly-thinker is left no choice but to get out of bed, retrieve Cutie Pie, and go down to the building lobby for a Bruce Society meeting.

I really want to ask Sue/Bruce, "Do you think Ely has ever seen Naomi naked?" but I don't. Because I'm sure he has. Gay guys get all the perks with none of the responsibility. It's so not fair.

I hate that I only got to see Naomi naked because last summer Ely was seeing some boy and Naomi hated not having full access to Ely's time so she gave me access to hers. And then Ely dumped the boy and Naomi dumped me.

Someone ought to dump something on *Ely*.

Did Naomi just walk by, barefoot and carrying a laundry load, or am I dreaming? I've got to be, because she is an insomniac's most dire and darling vision, wearing a tiny, tiny, dreamy, dreamy black dress, the kind she wears when she's going out partying with Ely, and it's got to be the highest form of injustice how Naomi does not realize that she could look like a dump truck for all that Ely would notice her in the way she wants him to notice her.

The highlight of Bruce Society meetings comes when Gabriel the doorman notices he has nothing to do after midnight. He leaves his station, walks over to our area, and dumps a deck of cards onto the coffee table in the middle of the square of lobby couches. "Five-card stud?" He sits down with us and shuffles the deck.

Our members dutifully pull the rolls of quarters from our pockets that serve in place of poker chips as Gabriel deals. Since he took over the night shift last June, I think it's fair to say that Gabriel has become a very rich guy. I don't know what kind of salary a novice doorman with no experience makes, but Gabriel could easily fund laundry loads lasting into eternity with all the quarters he's won.

Sue/Bruce asks, "I'm still waiting to hear from *you*, Gabriel, about when *you're* going to make college plans. I know you've

30

said you wanted to take some time off after high school, but how old are you now? Nineteen? Almost twenty? It's time, son. I'd be glad to write a recommendation letter for you. What schools interest you? Have you heard of Vassar?"

Like it's not obvious Ely put his mother up to gay-baiting Gabriel. *Vassar.* Right. A stud like Gabriel? So not gay, *Ely.* Keep on dreaming. Just like I dream of you being dipped in a vat of vinegar long enough so the smell permanently attaches to your skin and Naomi can't stand to be around you anymore. Skunk.

"Dunno." Gabriel shrugs.

Dunno? Dunno! This Bruce knows. Case solved: Gabriel the doorman, you are hereby proclaimed a Heterosexual. Make mine a Michelob, too, pal. You know what will also work? The beer that comes with the lederhosen girl whose breasts are spilling out of her uniform as she hands out the brewskis. Yeah.

Naomi would look awesome as the lederhosen beer girl. I bet she wouldn't wear panties underneath.

The Chihuahua barks from my lap, and believe me, my lap is relieved for the distraction. With a tail wag and puppy yelp, Cutie Pie indicates the lobby door, where a new person has arrived. We all look up to see the cause of the disturbance.

Bruce the Second stands at the lobby entrance. He looks as tired as I don't feel. Ruined. Or maybe that's how I want to see him. Really he just looks like Bruce the Second, the main difference being now he appears as confused as he is moronic. Gabriel Bruce the Doorman asks him, "Who are you here to see?"

It's like some psychic connection between Cutie Pie and me, because I'm sure her continued barking is really gossip code for "Check it over there, *papi*. Cuz don't you know about wha'happen'd?"

"I'm not sure," says Bruce the Second, fidgeting with the cell phone in his hand.

Excuse me? Everyone knows Naomi's mom is out by 11:00 p.m.—and hell hath no fury like a divorcée on anti-depressants who's awoken by a doorbell or the ring of her daughter's cell phone. Who else could other-Bruce be here to see?

I'm so not getting to sleep 'til I find out wha'happen'd.

KEY

It's 12:08 a.m. and I look hot. I mean, I should look hot, since I've spent the past hour working it. As Naomi always says, *I'd fuck me*. Of course, I always tell her, "Well, it's a good thing you're gonna fuck you, cuz it ain't gonna be me." She loves it. *Loves* it.

The door chime's ringing, and I can't believe that bitch is picking tonight of all nights to be only eight minutes late. If I'd known she would be this early-late, I would have told her twelve-thirty. Then I realize: She probably just wants to borrow something. No fucking way is Naomi ready before one.

I open the door and it's Bruce the Second.

"I was in the neighborhood," he says.

"No you weren't," I say, just joking.

He looks down at his feet, embarrassed.

Fuck.

"Well, I'm glad you weren't in the neighborhood," I say. "Come in."

I feel like Naomi's going to open her door at any moment, and I don't want that to happen.

It's not that she took the news badly. I said, "Hey, I kissed Bruce the Second," and she was all like, "Yeah, whatever." Then she said, "I hope you had a better time with him than I have."

And I actually kept my mouth shut. Because I didn't say, "Yeah, I probably did." Instead I pointed out that she'd never put him on the No Kiss List.

And she said, "Well, I didn't bother to put your grandma on the list, either. Some things are just obvious. Bruce the Second's not exactly your type."

I told her she was right. Because she was. Is. He's totally not my type.

Although lately, I have to say, my type has seemed to be total bullshit.

It's *Seventeen* that's letting me down, I tell you. Naomi and me both. I swear, we take those quizzes like they were sponsored by the College Board. *When the boy you like walks you to his car, does he: (a) go around and open the door for you, (b) get in the car and then lean over to unlock your door, (c) put you in the trunk, (d) sit you in the backseat and say, "Take off your clothes and I'll be with you in a second"?* Naomi and I were never satisfied with the answers, just like we were never satisfied by the kind of guys who would be photographed for *Seventeen*, looking so goofy in their board shorts that you had to know they were the managing editor's nephews or sons. We'd make up new quizzes for each other— *Would your ideal date be underwater or atop a sea of lava?*—

and the prize at the end would always be dinner for two at whatever restaurant we were walking toward. More often than not, we'd take the quizzes for each other. And we were almost always right.

Except the Bruce the Second Quiz. When she'd asked me, *Would you rather go out with: (a) a former First Lady, (b) gorillas in the mist, (c) a woman who looked like Stephen King, or (d) a future accountant,* I went with (b). But it's not the gorillas at my door now, is it?

I take Bruce the Second into the living room. He sits down on the couch. I offer him a drink. And then I'm like, whoa, we're returning to the scene of the crime, aren't we? But that wasn't the idea. Not mine. And it doesn't look like it's his, either. He doesn't seem to have the remotest clue about what he's doing.

"Are you sure you don't want to have a drink?" I offer. "I've already had two."

Truth: It's three, but since two of them were only about half as strong as the other one, I figure that counts as two. Usually it takes at least four for me to start feeling like life's a musical. And it takes at least five for me to start feeling like life's a disco musical. It's a very expensive habit, unless you happen to have very cheap taste.

"Bruce?" I ask. Because he's turned about as expressive as the couch he's sitting on. Which, incidentally, is beige floral. *Very* lesbian.

Lord, I shouldn't have kissed him. But, Lord, if You hadn't

wanted me to kiss him, why did You put him in my room like that?

"I'm sorry," Bruce says. He's turned away from me again, so it's like he's apologizing to the wall.

"What for?" I ask. It's a genuine question. I have no idea.

"For coming here so late. For wanting to see you."

"It's no problem," I say. "I was just about to go out anyway. So it's not like you woke me up."

I don't touch the "wanting to see you" part, because honestly it's setting off the Neediness Alarm in my head.

The door chime rings again. I hear Naomi scraping at the door, calling, "Let me in!" She doesn't really care if the moms are home—one of them loves her and the other one owes her. Conveniently Naomi forfeited her key to my apartment a few months ago, when we fought over whether it was wrong of me to give a sweater of hers to a boy I wanted to sleep with. She threw the key at me; I kept it. She asked for it back four days later, after I'd stolen the goddamn sweater from the boy's apartment, figuring he'd blame his hairy roommate. I kept both the sweater and the key, because I had to teach her to never throw a key at me again. With her aim and my luck, she'd end up poking out both of my eyes.

"C'mon," I tell Bruce. I grab his hand and pull him back to my bedroom. He seems to remember the way from yesterday. I figure I can just close him in there for a little while. But then I have one of those brilliant revelations that screams, *You. Are. A. Dumbfuck.* Because no way is Naomi coming into this apartment without pawing through my room for something.

So I tell Bruce to get into the closet. He does it, and as I stare at the closed door I think, *Did I really just tell Bruce to get into the closet? That is too fucking obvious on so many levels.*

Naomi is treating my apartment door like it's starring in the seventh sequel to *Saw,* and I know the assault won't compare to the barrage of questions I'll face if I don't open it in the next thirteen nanoseconds.

"Where the fuck were you?" she says as soon as she gets in the apartment.

"I was jerking off and you startled me so much I dropped the photo of you into the toilet," I say. "Calm down. You're acting like it's that time of the month and I'm the OPEC of tampons."

She looks good, but unfinished. I give her the once-over while she gives me the third degree. Neither of us needs a mirror when the other one's around.

"Is that my wristband? Are you ready to go? Why aren't you answering your door? Are you ever going to give me that key back?"

This is all precious, since any gay boy worth his Madonna singles could tell that she's come over to borrow a belt. Naomi hates hates hates the fact that we fit into the same jeans, but that doesn't stop her from treating my clothes like I only have them on loan from her.

"I'm going to wear the red one," I say. "I know I'm wearing this one right now, but I was about to change to the red one."

"Fuck you. You look hot and you know it. You're just saying the red one to throw me off the trail of your lick-my-hips-with-your-hands glitter belt. And I'm telling you, tonight that baby's calling this waist Mama."

There's no use arguing, especially since she's totally paying for my drinks tonight, whether she knows it (awwww, Ely's puppy dog eyes) or not (stupid waif still hates purses enough to ask me to hold her plastic wallet).

She bounds into my room, and I swear it's like I can hear the closet breathing. Bad move bad move bad move.

"Over here," I say, thanking the Lord that I'm too goddamn busy to ever get my used clothes beyond my desk chair.

I hand her the glitter belt.

"Looks better on me," I say.

"Only when it's fastening you to the bedpost," she shoots back.

Spoken like a true ignorant, which is what I love about my girl.

"All set?" I say.

"Do you mind if Bruce comes along?" Naomi asks. Clearly I balk, because she laughs and says, "What? He's downstairs. I needed clean underwear, okay? I went to the laundry room, and he was hanging out with the sleeplessheads in the lobby."

I'm so confused.

"The First," Naomi says. "Not your cheap-thrill kissing

partner. I swear, if he didn't have such good teeth, I'd let you have your little mindfuck for a little while longer."

"That's not fair," I say. The words are coming out before I can think, *Don't say that, foolboy.*

"Wait a sec." Naomi pauses right in front of the closet. "You make out with *my boyfriend* and *I'm* the one not being fair? Even a two-year-old on meth would be able to see how wrong that is."

"I meant *fair* in the *I have no fucking idea what I'm talking about* sense."

"Oh, I see. Maybe I need your leather jacket to compensate."

She reaches to pull open the closet door. I do the only thing I can think of to stop her.

"Yeah, if you want to look dumpy," I say.

Bingo.

"You think it makes me look dumpy?" She actually sounds hurt.

"Sweetheart, the damn thing makes *me* look dumpy. Why do you think I haven't been wearing it lately? I'm ready to give it back to the cow. Cuz at least the cow's *supposed to* look like a cow."

"Okay," she says, checking the mirror one more time. "Let's go."

I turn out the light as I leave my room, since I always do that and I don't want it to seem like anything's out of the ordinary. It's only once we're out in the foyer between our apartments that I say, "Oh fuck!"

"What?" Naomi asks.

"I forgot something. I'll be right back."

"What did you forget?"

"My dick, okay? You can't possibly expect me to go out without my dick! I'll be right back."

I close the door before she can get out another line. I run back to my room, open the closet, and see Bruce the Second standing there in the dark.

"I want you to stay," I say. "I'll come back as soon as I can."

He nods. But he doesn't look happy.

I figure it out.

"You're not a cheap thrill, and this isn't a mindfuck," I tell him. I don't know *what* it is, but at least I know it's not either of those.

He steps into the dark shadows of the room. He touches my shoulder. So damn earnest, and I so damn want to kiss him.

"I promise I won't be long," I say.

"Go," he tells me. "I'll be here."

I'm almost out the door when he says, "Gum."

"What?"

He throws me a pack of Orbit.

"Tell her you went back for gum."

"Thanks," I say. I could get used to a guy who knows his way around an alibi.

I head back through the apartment. Naomi's waiting outside in the elevator. I have no doubt she's been holding it this whole time. It strikes me for the gazillionth time that she is completely fucking beautiful. And I love it, because my love for her has absolutely nothing to do with that. I love her because she'll hold the elevator for me even if heading downstairs without me would make more of a point. I love her because if she sees a shirt that she knows will look good with my eyes, she'll buy it for me, even if she can't afford it. I love her because when I feel like putting my head in an oven, she'll gently take it out and bake me cookies instead. I love her because she can curse like a sailor and could no doubt sail like a sailor, too, if she put her mind to it. I love her because even though she doesn't always tell the truth, she always feels like she should. I love her because I don't need to love her all the time.

"Got your dick?" she asks.

"What do you care?" I say.

She snorts, hits the lobby button, and tells me, "All I know is that this party better not suck. If it does, you're going to be one dead Ducky."

I feel disloyal. Because as the elevator heads down, I feel like I'm moving away from something instead of toward something. The love I have for Naomi is the kind that's understood. But I feel compelled to go back to the thing I don't completely understand.

He'd go around and open the door for me, wouldn't he?

I can't let Naomi know what I'm thinking.

This is very treacherous ground.

ORBIT

"Got *your* dick, Naomi?" Ely smirks at me as the elevator goes down.

"If I did, would it get me anywhere with you?" He thinks he looks so hot in that red belt. It totally makes him look dumpy. Dumpy *and* red-hot flaming. *Very* tragic combination on a gay boy.

"Negative," Ely responds. He leans into me, jutting his chest against mine, then angles his face like he's going to kiss me. His lips are almost touching mine when his hand lands in between our mouths. "Gum?" he asks, twirling a pack between his fingers. Like a piece of gum will successfully overpower Ely's late-night ϒ scent. Ely will say it was only one, but his breath power indicates at least three.

A piece of olive is lodged in between his two front teeth. It gives his face a most welcome ugly appeal. If Ely leans in any closer to me, the friction between his smile and my anticipation would be like a 💣 begging to detonate.

I do realize a big bad 🌍 is happening out there—war and injustice and global warming and all that hope and

humanity—but I'm sorry, I care most about the Naomi &
Ely ⸘bubble⸘. It's what's gotten me through this far in life. It
doesn't burst. Like everything else does.

I place my index finger inside my mouth so he'll know
about the olive. He immediately licks it from his teeth.

Ten . . . nine . . . eight . . .

He's so close already—why not?

"Time-out?" I tease, referring to our occasional hands-
free, means-nothing-but-platonic-love-between-best-friends
make-out sessions that don't count in real time. (The time-outs
only happen when we're drinking or bored—which interest-
ingly seem to go hand in hand, or mouth to mouth, as the case
may be.)

"You're only using me for my gum," he teases back.
"How can I trust you'll still respect me in the morning?"

He pulls back, dances around me, playful.

False alarm. I lied. There's no 💣, and Ely doesn't look
dumpy or red-hot flaming. He just looks like Ely. He's not hot,
like Gabriel. He's Ely. Lovely. The first person I think of when
I wake up in the morning, the last person I hope for when I fall
asleep at night. The one person who's as much a part of me
as me.

Maybe I'm an egoist. I'm not sure exactly what an egoist
is, but I'd appreciate any label right now that could clarify exactly what Ely and I are. To each other.

I mean, I know we know. But *do* we really know?

The egoist version of us distills Naomi & Ely, two parts of
the same whole. My mom and his moms have 🔊 me over and

over again that sexual preference is not a choice, but when Ely's leaning and teasing, so close to me without touching me, yet I still *feel* him—up here, down there, on every centimeter of my skin—it's like I can't , because no matter what anyone says, I can't help but believe that *he* chose for *me*:

Naomi   Ely

When we were thirteen and learning how to kiss by using each other as practice, *gay* wasn't even an issue. It felt so natural and sweet and right. No wall existed between us, because it was so clear we were destined to share that first experience together. His lips didn't feel *gay* then. Why should they now? Just because Ely is attracted to boys doesn't mean he couldn't want to push our mind-meld into body-meld. I refuse to believe it's possible he couldn't want that, too, on some level, whether he knows it or not.

Or maybe, as backup friend the girl Robin advises, I've known Ely too long and too well, and my eyes only see what my heart projects.

I need to spend more time with other girls.

The elevator door opens.

Ely places a piece of gum into my palm as we step into the lobby hall area. I stop cold.

Bruce the Second really does have great teeth—bright and shiny, perfectly straight, almost works of art. The art is no accident. Both his parents are dentists. They allegedly own the mouths of the LIRR Ronkonkoma Branch Line's elite. And their prodigal good son chews only sugar-free gum. Bruce the Second is an Orbit man. Ely is Dentyne's bitch.

"Since when do you chew Orbit?" I ask Ely. I do not unwrap the gum. I pop a Tic Tac into my mouth instead, from my own stash.

"Since Madonna started writing children's books. Why do you care?"

I step back from him, resisting the urge to shove him against the wall. ☠ Naomi, come out, come out, wherever you are.

I care because, um, oh yeah, BRUCE THE SECOND IS MY BOYFRIEND! Or was. Or something. I mean, I don't think I really care that Bruce is about to not be my boyfriend anymore, unless he's already not my boyfriend and we're so indifferent we're not even bothering with an official breakup scene. I do care about the fact of my best friend being the reason for that. Maybe when Ely confessed he'd kissed Bruce the Second, I was like, "Yeah, whatever." That indifference was a lie. It's like when Ely says, "Well, it's a good thing you're gonna fuck you, cuz it ain't gonna be me," and I laugh. Indifference lies to protect my hurt.

In order to stay in Ely's orbit, you have to make choices. *Yes, Ely, you really do have a chance with Heath Ledger. No, Ely, no one thinks you're an asshole when you fall down drunk on the pavement and your friends have to carry you home. You're fun Fun FUN! Ely,* of course *I'm teasing you about wanting to sleep with you. Why would I want to ruin our friendship like that?* You have to choose to let Ely believe his fantasy version of reality, for the sake of preserving Naomi & Ely.

Fuck Ely for making me crawl through his Ely-⬠ to survive our friendship.

But if I crawl out, where can I go? What's left? Ely can spin and weave and dart and aim with other boys all he wants, so long as I've remained his cen◉ter. His queen.

I can't believe I'm pushing this.

"Why'd you really go back to your apartment?" I ask Ely. "Cuz I saw your dick the first time out of the apartment and Dicky was like, *Mmmm, girl, you and me, we're going to have us a good ol' time at Ducky's tonight.*"

"Gum," Ely says.

Bingo.

I lie all the time, but I hate being lied to.

👂 👂 👂

If only Bruce the Second had been a Wrigley's gum-chewer, and not an Orbit man. Four out of five dentists can basically guarantee that their sons who chew Wrigley's turn out to be straight; odds are three out of five dentists would at least reassure a straight girl patient that their sons will stay in the closet where they belong until they've figured out their sexuality for sure. No need to place those sons' names on a No Kiss List™.

Bruce the Not My Boyfriend Anymore has no idea the jeopardy he's jumping into. I sort of feel sorry for him. He probably has no idea that when it comes to boy prey, Ely is all about the hunt but doesn't give a shit about the capture. And I'm not going to be the ❶ to warn him. ❶ time on the ❶ train I tried to warn Bruce the ❷ about me, but we ended up making out instead. I'd rate our chemistry a 👎. Bruce can figure Ely out for himself. Good luck.

Keep moving, Naomi. Don't react. Don't give it all away.

As Ely and I approach the lobby seating area, where the sleeplessheads congregate, I check myself out in the lobby mirror. God, I *am* so pretty. What a waste, if Ely doesn't notice—at least, notice my looks in the Wow-Naomi-is-boner-hot way, and not in the Wow-those-stilettos-I-picked-out-for-Naomi-go-great-with-her-dress way. Truth: If my little black dress looks amazing on this body, it's because my waist wears *his* belt around it. If my face shines, the glow is Ely by my side.

Ely is probably right. The best I'll ever get is if I fuck me. In fact, I've tried, but masturbation turns out to be hella time-consuming with not very satisfactory results. Or maybe I'm just doing it wrong. My work ethic has always been weak.

I've never understood why looking hot has to be equated with sex and conquest. Whatever happened to anticipation, to courtship, to true love? Can't a person look hot and not have it mean something? Call me an old-fashioned Naomi bitch, but I'm holding out for true love. Even if it is an unattainable fantasy.

I'm not going to make the mistake of letting beauty (mine or his) guide my attraction to any man. That love-at-first-sight crap does *not* work. My father saw my mother's picture in a

47

magazine and fell for her before he'd even met her. When I was little, he would spend more time photographing her than photographing the images that were supposed to be supporting our family. But his attachment to her looks could only be sustained so long. Dad eventually tossed aside the beauty myth for the very real lesbian across the hall. He even wanted to leave Mom for her, but then the lesbian remembered she was a lesbian after all, so Dad just left, and Mom decided to cover her beauty under her bedcovers.

I don't think it was Dad choosing a lesbian over her that most damaged Mom's sense of her own femininity. I think it was losing her marriage to a woman she'd called "friend."

The poker players halt their game when Ely and I reach their area of the lobby. We pause at the same time to silently admire Gabriel, dealing cards to the sleeplessheads. Yeah, I'd have *him*—who wouldn't?—but he's ranked number two on the No Kiss List™, and I UNDERSTAND THE BOUNDARIES.

Sue knows trouble when she sees it. "Naomi, does your mother know you're going out so late?" I suspect it's my outfit that concerns Sue, not the hour.

"Yes," I lie. My mother's passed out in the pharmaceutical daze she's been in since Dad left. The doctor finally cut off her sleeping pill supply, but Bruce the First didn't know that when he gave her his stash in exchange for Mom doing his laundry after his sister went on strike and told him to stop being a big baby and learn to do his own damn laundry.

I do Mom's laundry, too, now. I don't mind. She's very good about separating her whites from her colors. But no matter how many laundry loads I do for her or dinners I prepare for her or nights I spend curled up in bed next to her, I just can't shake the blue out of her. I wish I could be that gold-standard daughter.

Mr. McAllister stands up from the leather couch, clutching last month's *Vogue*. Pervert. " 'Night, all," he says, taking a bow before walking over and stepping into the elevator.

"Wait!" I call out to him.

The elevator door opens back up. I turn to Ely. "Are you sure you didn't leave anything else up in your apartment?"

He so looks guilty. I so want to hate him.

"Like what?" Ely mumbles.

"Like your balls, to go along with your dick?"

"Language, young lady!" Sue scolds, gesturing in the direction of sweet Bruce the First with Mrs. Loy's Chihuahua in his lap. High school boys. So fresh, so clean. So pathetic and yet so irresistible. He breaks my heart for breaking his heart. I kill me.

Well, then. Distraction, thank you so very, very much for seating yourself in the lobby in the middle of the night. No, not *that* distraction. Gabriel's major league, and I might not look it but I am still farm team. Attention: pinch hitter. Bruce the First, step up to the plate, please.

Ely can buy his own damn drinks tonight. A girl who looks like me should not be such a □. It's time for a changing of the guard. Why shouldn't the □ be a ♦ instead, or any^{thing} or any[1] to help me escape the lie of ◎?

"What are you saying, Naomi?" Ely asks.

"Are you coming or not?" Mr. McAllister bellows from inside the elevator.

"Not!" Ely responds. The elevator door closes.

My mouth opens in honesty—long overdue. "I'm saying I hope you have a good time tonight with whatever it is you're not telling me about. Because I changed my mind. Girl's prerogative. C'mon, Bruce. Let's take Cutie Patootie out for a walk. You and me. I don't want to go to that stupid NYU party with you, Ely."

Stupid NYU parties, that's what got us into this situation in the first place. Last fall, our first semester at NYU, we went to a party at the Robins' dorm. Ely and I were the hit of the *High School Musical* sing-and-bong-along crowd as we sang "Breakin' Free" together. Our routine was well rehearsed— we'd performed the leads in our own high school senior musical the previous spring, me cast as Troy, and Ely cast as Gabriella. But that night, as I danced and sang Troy's part, "We're breaking free!" when Ely as Gabriella was supposed to twirl and sing out "We're soaring!" and together we'd sing "Flying!" all of a sudden Ely flew away instead of singing, just like that. Some real Troy look-alike had caught his eye and demanded his immediate attention.

People think beauty is a blessing, but sometimes it's not— like at college parties, when your gay best friend dumps you for a cute boy, and every other guy there is too intimidated to talk to you. That's where Bruce the Second came in. Later he told me he didn't think he'd ever have a shot with a girl like me, so why not take a chance on talking to her?

Become her friend? He sat down next to me as I sulked over Ely's abandonment. He said, "You know, people think Ginger Rogers was Fred Astaire's favorite dance partner. But that's not true. He always said his favorite partner was Rita Hayworth."

I must have been really drunk not to have gotten it right then and there.

"I always thought his favorite was Cyd Charisse," I slurred. I'd never seen one Fred Astaire dance movie; I was merely repeating something my grandmother had once said. Not like that stopped me from talking on the Fred/Ginger/Rita/Cyd—and who the *fuck* is Gene Kelly, anyway?—topic with Bruce for maybe fifteen minutes. Then I couldn't take it anymore. The boring subject. I grabbed on to this Bruce; time for distractionary making out.

What can I say? I liked Bruce the Second the accounting major. He added up to easy boyfriend. No pressure. No expectations. He was always available when Ely wasn't.

And I know it's like I should be furious with Ely now, and wondering if I was just Bruce the Second's gay learning curve, but even as I'm about to take off with Bruce the First, really what I'm feeling is *Please, Bruce the Second, please. Don't take Ely away from me.*

"You've got to be kidding me," Ely says. "Even for you, Naomi, this is outrageous. You're going to stand here wearing my belt and tell me you'd rather go out with Bruce the First and that stupid fucking dog?"

The other side of me is thinking, *Go back upstairs, Ely.*

Fuck off and fly away. Find what you're looking for, who's so clearly not me. I wanted you to be my first, Ely, and you laughed at me. I held off Bruce the Second when he tried to be my first, not only because I wondered if he only wanted to do it with me just to prove that he could but because I wanted that first time to be special. Shared with someone I love rather than someone I like. It didn't have to mean you wouldn't be gay or I was in *love with you. It wouldn't mean I was just trying to get back at Ginny cuz the only thing she'd hate more than you getting it on with a girl would be you getting it on with a girl who happens to be related to my dad.*

"Yes," I tell Ely. I hope the word sounds like a slap. "And don't curse in front of the children." I cannot believe we are having a conversation this fucking stupid. I cannot believe I am pushing it farther still. "And how do you know Cutie Patootie is fucking stupid? Is there some IQ test for Chihua—"

"It's Cutie Pie, not Patootie," Bruce the First interrupts. He bounces up from his chair. The dog barks, tail wagging, eager for a trot outside.

Bruce the First. *First.* I'm going to show that boy a good time tonight. And it's not going to be some superficial good time that's all about pink cocktails and pretty boys and getting laid. There will be no party tonight, there will be no imbibing or ritual dancing to Madonna and Kylie Minogue songs as if I like them, and there will be no Naomi & Ely adventure. I'm taking Bruce and that dog somewhere instead, don't know where yet, but somewhere nice and wholesome. Maybe a Bible study group for insomniacs. Maybe roller-skating at the under-18 club. Maybe to girl-Robin's dorm to play Pictionary. We're going to act our mean age—not our inflated, sophisticated Manhattan age.

This city is so fast. Ely is so fast. My heartbeat is so fast. I want to slow down.

"Just so we both clearly understand the stand you are taking, Naomi, I'm going to ask you this once and only once. Do you *really* not want to go out with me tonight? Or are you lying?" Ely asks.

"No." I'm lying. About what, I'm not sure.

One thing I'm absolutely sure of. Step aside, Donnie Weisberg, wherever you are, and make way for a new name on the No Kiss List™: Ely.

The winner, as always.

KNOCKDOWN

Last time I offer her gum—I'll tell you that.

Here I was, thinking we had all these pillars of our friendship in a row. Only it ends up that they're dominoes. And all it takes is a pack of gum to send 'em tipping over.

She's lying. I know she's lying. But if she's not going to admit that she's lying, it's just as bad.

Domino. Domino. Domino.

"You're lying," I say.

Domino.

"So are you," she says back.

Domino.

"Guys?"

"Yes, Bruce," Naomi asks, clearly annoyed. I take some consolation that it's not only me.

Cutie Pie starts barking up a storm. Maybe all this lying's made her want to pee.

"Nothing," Bruce the First says.

Cutie Pie's now acting like King Kong's blowing a dog whistle.

"You see," Naomi says, "even Cutie Patootie knows you're lying."

"Cutie Pie," Bruce corrects again. And for a millisecond there, I actually like him. He never stands up for himself, but at least he stands up for the dog.

Naomi lets out this pout-snort that's like her impersonating Madonna impersonating the Queen of England.

Cutie Pie's straining at his leash, pulling for the door. And I swear Naomi's looking at him like he's telling her things about me.

"You're acting weird, Naomi," I say.

"And you're just plain *acting*, Ely," she says back.

This from the girl who was a drama queen before we were old enough to go to Dairy Queen.

I have no desire to see the night crash to the ground. I want to go out, have a good time, appease Naomi, and get back to Bruce in my bedroom. I don't see any reason why I can't do all of these things.

"Look," I say, "is this about Bruce?" I figure we might as well talk about it instead of using all our energy to avoid it.

"What about me?" Bruce-who's-downstairs-with-us asks.

"Not you," Naomi says. "The other one."

Bruce seems a little pleased that he's the primary Bruce.

"Is he coming, too?" he asks.

"Why don't you ask Ely?" Naomi says, both bitter and brittle. Britter.

"Can we just go?" I say.

But Bruce the First is still inspecting the starting block.

"Wait—what's going on?" he asks, dumbwildered. "Isn't he here with you, Naomi? I saw him go upstairs."

Oh Lord. Just my luck he chooses this moment to be Encyclopedia Brown.

"Is that right, Bruce?" Naomi says. She looks like she's about to pet him.

"Naomi—" I start.

"Yeah, he came in a few minutes ago," Bruce continues.

"Look, Naomi—" I offer again. There are very few situations that can't be saved with an explanation.

But Naomi isn't going to let me continue.

"Well," she huffs, "it looks like it's Colonel Bastard in Ely's bedroom with a candlestick. Or is it a bludgeon, Ely?"

"I'm not really sure I'm following you two," Bruce says.

At least Cutie Pie, quiet now, seems to have pieced it together. He doesn't want to miss a word.

"Look," I say, "I was going to go out with you anyway. He can wait. You're my top priority."

"Oh, that's brilliant, Ely. That's just *super.* I'm so *flattered* that you'd put my needs over the needs of *my boyfriend.*"

Okay, if we're going to start using kneejerks to knock down the dominoes, allow me to add:

"Well, *Naomi,* I think it's safe to say he's not your boyfriend anymore."

Naomi smacks her forehead. "Well, gee, how stupid of me to think that *someone would let me know.*"

Oh, enough already. "You know none of us meant for this to happen. It's like the whole Devon Knox thing."

"Ely, *DEVON KNOX WAS STRAIGHT.* Your crush didn't count. And that was *THREE YEARS AGO.*"

"He was on the list."

"I forgot, okay?"

Cue: Inspector Bruce.

"What's happened?" he asks.

"Look, Bruce, could you just leave us alone for a second?"

Okay, so the city has 311 for you to call to ask for repairs and shit, and 411 to get people's phone numbers, and 911 to call the police or the fire department or paramedics. Well, I propose they add 711, so if you find yourself stuck in the lobby of an apartment building with an irrationally tirading best friend and her unbuff buffoon of an ex (and a hot doorman looking on), you can dial three simple digits and they can send a calm, sane person to help you explain what's going on. Right now, my best bet is the dog, and he seems to need to pee again.

"Okay," Original Bruce says to Cutie Pie in an oopsy-woopsy voice. "Brucie's gonna take you out for a wee-wee."

Cutie Pie looks like he's going to rip Bruce's throat out for talking to him this way. I can't say I blame him. I've lost erections to vocal mannerisms like that.

I'm so absorbed in the dog's resistance that I almost don't hear Naomi say, "Ely, I can't do this anymore."

Here we go. Moment of truth.

I look her right in the eye. She turns to the side, so I scoot over and face her there.

I know she doesn't want to hear this. But I have to say it anyway.

"Naomi, I like him. I really do."

There. It's out there.

And she doesn't believe a word of it.

"Is that why you're hiding him?" she asks. "Because you like him so much?"

"You really want to know why I'm hiding him?"

"Why?" she asks.

I wish she hadn't.

Why?

"Because I'm afraid of you."

It's true. I am. Always have been.

"Well, I'm fucking afraid of you, too."

We stare at each other for a second.

Bruce jumps in. "Look, you two . . . maybe you should just cool off for a second."

"SHUT UP, BRUCE!" we both yell.

Well, at least we agree on something.

Hurt, Bruce starts pulling Cutie Pie away.

"C'mon, Cutie," Bruce says. "Let's go. I guess we're not wanted here."

Oh great—now the wittle boy's feewings are hurt.

"I'm coming with you," Naomi says. "I wanna dance with somebody who loves me."

Shit, girl—I pour out the truth of my heart and you're going to use *Whitney* against me?

"HAVE FUN!" I yell after them.

All the dominoes are down. No word back. Just the echo of Gabriel the hot midnight doorman wishing them a hot goodnight as they leave. Then the door closing. The elevator behind me making its way up to someone else's floor. The otherwise silence.

It takes me a second to remember that Bruce is waiting in my closet.

And that I like him.

VELMA

Here's what I love about big-city folk. They'll show up at your dorm room in the middle of the night, slurping cones from 31 Flavors in one hand and cradling sleeping Chihuahuas in the other, asking if you want to play Pictionary in the study lounge, like that's normal. In Schenectady, I assure you, this doesn't happen. In Schenectady, you have two parents (male/female), who generally stay together, and who would freak if their kid's school friend showed up at their home in the middle of the night. The big-city girl arrives under the guise of playing a board game, but really she's there to replay the epic smackdown scene that may have cost this girl her best friend. Oh, don't forget the part about the big-city girl bringing along he who looks like a farm boy, with the body of the Hulk and the face of that kid from *A Christmas Story* who gets his tongue stuck on the icy pole.

I knew it would be exciting to move to New York City, I knew it would be worth the second mortgage Mom and Dad had to take out on the house to finance my NYU education, but I didn't know it would take waiting until sophomore year for interesting things to finally happen. Freshman year was avoiding keggers and watching half of the Long Island / New Jersey diaspora go wild in their first year of freedom-from-parents. I merely observed this freshman madness. I am the Velma. I am the girl with the bowl haircut and the sensible sweater—the investigator, not the cause of investigation. I am not the thinnest, the prettiest, the coolest, or the loudest. I blend in easily, as should a girl from Schenectady. I am the girl whose freshman year was responsible and dean's list–worthy, the girl who spent her time studying, joining the school newspaper, and learning the difference between, say, a wacky-but-cute NYU *guy* named Robin who's worth engaging in conversation in Washington Square Park and just plain wack jobs who only want to sell you dope or Jesus in Washington Square Park. Basic stuff.

But then came sophomore year. That's when the girl from Schenectady met Naomi from West Ninth Street. She didn't have to go wild her first year of college. She grew up in the heart of Greenwich Village. Freshperson madness would be too old-school for her. She's seen it all, done it all. I'm pretty certain.

Here's why I feel sad for her, though. Naomi's so city-girl tough, she won't allow herself to cry, even though it's obvious she really wants to. Instead she reclines on the worn-out sofa in the study lounge, licking the sprinkles off her Jamoca Almond Fudge ice cream scoop, with a dog named Cutie Pie or Cutie Patootie, I'm not sure, taking what appears to be a much-needed nap on her stomach. Which is shaking from

Naomi's sob-avoidance, or just appears to be from the dog's vibration. Naomi stares blankly at the ceiling while her latest appendage, who actually answers to "Bruce the First," sits in a chair opposite her, assuring her the fight was Ely's fault. He has a Pink Bubblegum flavor cone in his one hand and uses the remote control in his other hand to switch between sports score rundowns on ESPN and some late-night *Dr. Phil* replay. He has some involuntary twitching problem every time the word *Ely* is uttered.

Awesome. I love New York.

"So does this mean you and the other Bruce are officially broken up now?" I ask Naomi. That guy was both too nice and too boring for a girl like Naomi. She's way out of his league. It's interesting, since that's the type she appears to go for. Guess that's what happens when the only guy you want is the only guy who won't have you.

I don't bother with dating. There is the problem of no one actually asking me on a date, but I choose not to think of that problem as a *problem*. It's a *solution*. The Velmas of the world do not intern at CNN, hope to be accepted at Columbia J-School after graduating NYU with honors, and go on to win Pulitzer Prizes by getting bogged down in relationship drama. That's a problem for the Daphnes of the world. Daphne, you bitch, you can't even drive the damn van.

"I guess so," Naomi mutters. Her jaw clenches, trying to stifle a sob, and I want to grab her hand and tell her everything will be okay, only her hands are occupied by ice cream and dog, and truthfully, I *don't* think everything will be okay for her and Ely. "Definitely," she adds. "Of course. Bruce the Second is history." An involuntary tear streams down her face, and I know that tear's name is "Ely" and not "Bruce the Second."

"Hey, Bruce the First," I say, which sounds so funny coming from my mouth. Nobody in Schenectady ever called someone a name like that. At least not on my street. I'm so glad I didn't go home this weekend, even though I'm really missing Mom's lasagna and Dad's boastful griping about my tuition bill. "I'm a Robin, and I'm friends with this film student guy, also named Robin. Isn't that neat?"

"*Neat?*" he asks me. "*Neat?* Where are you from, anyway?"

"Schenectady!"

"Crazy!" he says. I'm not sure if he's being rude or he just doesn't like any attention that's not focused on Naomi. I *am* sure his tone suggests an awful lot of hubris for a high school junior boy hanging out in the middle of the night in an NYU dorm, even for a mere high school junior who grew up on West Ninth Street.

"Leave us," Naomi commands Bruce the First.

So much for his hubris. Bruce the First jumps to his feet and grabs for the dog. "I think I'm finally ready to fall asleep."

"Are you still here, Bruce the First?" Naomi snaps, sitting up and pointing at the door. "DID I NOT JUST SAY 'LEAVE US'?"

He's gone like that and I must probe Naomi deeper. "And Ely says he's scared of you? Huh, go figure."

Now, alone with me, she cries. She sputters. "Ely . . . betrayal . . . how could he kiss a Bruce? . . . he's all I've ever had . . . no, Ely, not Bruce Two!, who cares about that Bruce? . . . I'm all alone now . . . I knew it would happen eventually . . . how could we survive our parents and my lies and his complete lack of desire for me and my complete not lack of it, but still . . . fuck . . . [sob sob sob] . . . I love him, friend or brother or whatever shade of Ely . . . sure we've gotten in fights before, but this is different . . . it just *is,* Robin . . . it's like a sacred trust that's broken . . . [sob sniffle sob sniffle] . . . don't you have a Kleenex-brand tissue, cuz this generic one you have here is really harsh on the skin . . . no, I'm not lying . . . [real Kleenex found and offered to her, snort and blow, sob sob, snort and blow] . . . thanks, Robin . . . you're the closest friend I have left now . . . Naomi & Ely—we're lost to each other now."

I really should text-message that other Robin about Naomi's presence here tonight; he wants to make a documentary about her and call it *Hot Child in the City,* but the real-time footage of her at this moment would be too sad and vulnerable and potentially flamingly soap-operatic, so I don't. Instead I sit down next to Naomi and let her cry it out onto my shoulder. There, there, city girl. Gosh, her hair smells good. It's weird, because Velmas aren't supposed to have this kind of *problem,* but my heart pounds a little harder with Naomi pressed against me, and it's not like I have any desire to be one of those college-girl experimental lesbians, but Naomi does have some magnetic effect on people. I can understand why that other Robin chases her for film footage and not me. Fascinating.

Name-twin powers truly can activate—the shape of he-

Robin stands at the lounge entrance as if he knew me-Robin was summoning him. He's wearing that blue Hawaiian shirt that makes me feel like I can almost smell the flowers pictured on it. The husky, sweet, imaginary scent those flowers give off could almost inspire a Velma to flip out into some very Daphne-style drunken antics. *Aloha.*

" 'Sup?" he asks.

How strange. My mouth feels parched and water is not going to cut it right now, because what I crave is *taste.* It's probably for the better that I am not a party girl and the only fizzy drink I can stomach is ginger ale. Back home there is this place called the Lost Dog Café that makes the awesomest ginger ale, with like fresh ginger. You have to drive all the way to Binghamton to get it, but it's completely worth the trip.

He-Robin's eyes investigate the room. "Where's your other half, anyway?" he asks Naomi. "Isn't it like some law that if you're out and about in the middle of the night, the Ely appendage is with you?" His blue eyes, lit by shirt, light up bluer still, sparked by idea. "Hey, I know people on the twelfth floor. You just say the word and I will get the karaoke machine down here for you and Ely to do *High School Musical* again." He holds up his text pager. "I know the people and I've got the necessary accessories, if you know what I'm saying, to get a scene happening in here."

Say yes, Naomi, I think, *please say yes. With the other Robin here, there's a wild and amazing party just waiting to happen.*

"No way," Naomi says. "Lame-ass parties in this dorm building are what started all the trouble in the first place."

Darn.

Robin snorts. "No one from Bruce's floor has ever figured out how a girl like you ended up making out with an econ major like him at that party here last semester."

"He's an accounting major," Naomi corrects.

"Dude, you don't even know your own boyfriend. Bruce is an econ major with a *possible* minor in accounting. He hasn't decided yet. He's also intrigued by anthropology."

"Dude," Naomi shoots back. "Guess I don't have to give a fuck, seeing as how Bruce is not my boyfriend anymore."

"Makes sense." Robin nods knowingly. "You're way out of his league. Everyone said so. But seriously, I hope there's not some trickle-down negative aftershock of depression if you dumped him, because I was going to hit Bruce up to help me study for my—"

"Shut the fuck up, Robin," Naomi says. "Can you not see I'm in mourning? Show some fucking sensitivity."

God, I love Naomi. She talks to boys so easily. I don't know how she does it. She's like a miracle worker.

"Knew I shoulda brought my Super 8 downstairs," Robin mutters. "Naomi mourning Bruce. Woulda been classic."

"Mourning Ely. ELY!" Her flip-out moment ends with the vibration of her cell phone. She wipes the tears from her face, embarrassed, then opens the phone. She looks up at me. Mood stabilized. "Text message. From Gabriel the hot doorman." That doorman *is* a fine specimen of hunk, even to a Velma like me, who normally wouldn't notice such endowment, I mean such shallow observation of one man's resemblance to either of those main guys from Aerosmith (not the drummer, the other two), who both simply ooze sexual appeal no matter how geriatric they get. I could aspire to be a Daphne if I thought it would attract the likes of either of them to me, or that Gabriel guy, or even the other Robin guy. I'd be a Daphne from *Albany* for any of those guys. Crazy!

"You text-message with your *doorman*?" I ask Naomi. I might officially worship her now.

"Yeah, but don't tell Ely. Gabriel's currently number two on the No Kiss List."

Tears, welcome back.

"You gonna be okay?" I ask Naomi, pulling her into another embrace.

She nods onto my bosom, I mean my sensible sweater, stifling a sniffle. Then she looks up at me, goddess face, resplendent in the glow of tear-stained cheeks. "Gabriel's shift just ended, and he's headed over to some club on Avenue B. He's in this band called The Abe Froman Experience. Their set's gonna start in about an hour. That's gotta be a better diversion than any dorm party that could be brewing here."

A Velma is obligated to remind Naomi, "I thought you wanted to slow down."

"*Vrrroooommmm,*" Naomi answers. "Wanna go, Robins?"

DO I!

Awesome.

MUTANT

What am I doing in this closet?

Surely, when Ely told me not to leave, he didn't mean to stay in here.

Right?

After a good two minutes (I count to 120), I step out. I don't close the door behind me, though. I look in and see all of Ely's pretty shirts. They look like they're made of wrapping paper.

I shop at the Gap. I don't even have the body for Abercrombie's non-muscle wear. I own three pairs of jeans and rotate them. (For those, I splurged and went to Banana Republic.) What am I doing here?

I know Ely's not toying with me. I trust him. But I also feel that *life* is toying with me. This can't be right. The Cosmic Screenwriter is doing this as a joke.

Ely would never fall for a guy wearing a Gap button-down and Banana Republic jeans. Especially not L, 34/32.

And I would never fall for a guy who was . . . well . . .

68

a guy. That was the script, right? I mean, I'm all for falling for the person, not the gender . . . but this is not exactly where I thought I'd be. I won't lie: I've definitely thought about the guy thing before. And then I've dismissed it. Until this. This won't be dismissed.

I know I should leave. Just go. Because there's a point where a mistake turns into a big mistake, and I should probably come to my senses before I get there.

But of course, *come to my senses* makes no sense. My senses are happy here. Or they will be, when he comes back.

I wonder if I should still be hiding. I crouch down to look under the bed, to see if maybe I could fit there.

And that's how I find it.

The mother lode.

At first I don't get it. I see all the plastic sleeves, and since the lode's under the bed, my first reaction is, *He keeps his porn in mint condition?*

Then I reach in and pull one out.

It can't be.

But it is. It looks like he has every single X-Men comic published in the last ten—no, twenty—years. None of the desperate spin-offs. Just the core series. Wolverine. Jean Grey. Emma Frost. Mmmm . . . Emma Frost.

The X-Men were pivotal heroes for me. Before them, I always liked the more conventional superheroes, the ones like Superman and Batman, who had their "normal" alter egos—

their Clark Kent and Bruce Wayne lives to hide behind. But the X-Men were different. They were always exactly who they were. Wolverine couldn't shave himself and put on a tie and go to work at a newspaper. Rogue couldn't touch anyone, whether she was at school or at war. Cyclops couldn't change out of a cape and attend fancy dinner parties. No, the mutants were full-time mutants. Their powers and their weaknesses were all out in the open.

That appealed to me.

I was never allowed to collect comics. My mother didn't like the clutter. She said I should donate my old comics to poor children who didn't have any comics of their own to read. How could I argue with that?

Ely, clearly, has a different philosophy.

I leave the comics in their plastic sleeves. I can't violate them with my fingerprints. Not without asking.

But I look at the covers, all the Jim Lee scenes, so many different shades of mutant. There are even star stickers stuck onto a few of the sleeves. Ely's favorites, no doubt.

I never would have guessed. Underneath the wrapping paper, there's an X-Men heart. Uncanny.

I'm so transfixed that I don't hear the footsteps or the door opening. But I sense a presence in the room, because I look up from my side of the bed and see one of Ely's moms hovering over it.

"Hello," she says. She does not seem particularly startled to see me.

"Hey," I say, starting to stand up.

"No, no—you can stay there. I'm sure you're just waiting for Ely. Make yourself comfortable."

And that's it. She turns around and leaves.

Which makes me wonder if this happens a lot.

Which makes me wonder why I'm still here.

I mean, I know Ely's slept with a lot of guys. Naomi has certainly mentioned what a boyslut he is. Whenever we were together, she boasted on his behalf. Not just the sex part. Everything. The boys, I sensed, were disposable. Naomi was granite. And Ely was granite to her. There was no way for me to compete with that. So I let her talk. I always let her talk. Mostly about Ely.

Do all the boys feel like this? I mean, is this the way it usually goes?

It's like I'm joining a club. The Boys Who've Fallen For Ely Club. Hundreds throughout the greater metropolitan area. Every year they have a potluck and compare their broken hearts.

How long do they usually wait for him in situations like this? An hour? Two? The whole night?

I'm not even supposed to like boys.

But, yeah. Here I am.

I lie down on the floor. Close my eyes. I can hear a television in another room—maybe his moms', maybe from the apartment downstairs. If I can hear them, can they hear me? I'm really nothing but a heartbeat and thoughts right now. Not restful or restless. The rest.

"You could use the bed, you know."

I open my eyes, and Ely is smiling over me. So damn sexy that I can't help but love it and fear it and resent it and want it.

"What time is it?" I ask. Did I fall asleep? Am I really awake?

"I've only been gone about ten minutes," he answers. "Miss me?"

I just say it. "Yes." Like that.

Please may this not be a game. Please may this not be a game. Because if it's a game, I know I'm going to lose.

I sit up and he sits down next to me. His breath smells like Orbit. He looks a little sad, but he's trying to hide it from me.

"Where's Naomi?" I ask.

"She left without me. Made a date with Bruce the First."

This is news. If you separate two people who are usually as fused together as an atom, there's bound to be an explosion.

But Ely's keeping it muted.

"I see you found the stash," he says, gesturing beneath the bed.

"It's *awesome*," I tell him.

I've entered the land of Bonus Points.

"You're into X-Men?" he asks, putting whatever's going on with Naomi aside in order to be with me.

"Are you kidding?" I tell him. "When I was nine, I actually mailed in an application to go to Xavier's school. Put a stamp on the envelope, put it in a mailbox—everything. I didn't hear from them, but the next year I did it again. And again."

"Their queer quota is probably full up."

I feel a little weird about him saying that—I don't think he realizes what new territory this is for me.

"I'm not sure I would've put that on the application then," I tell him. "But, yeah, maybe they have ways of knowing."

Ely looks at me in a way that feels like he's touching me.

"And how else are you a mutant?" he asks.

Sometimes attraction is the only truth serum you need. "I dunno," I begin. But I do know, and I'm going to tell him. "I'm afraid of the number six. I have a microscopic third nipple, which would have made me a witch in medieval times. I can roll my tongue. I'm unable to throw a Frisbee, no matter how hard I try. I avoid red foods."

"Even foods that have a little red in them?"

"No. They have to be all red. Pizza's okay, tomatoes—not so much."

He nods sagely. "I see."

I'm glad that he sees. But what I really wish he'd see is how much I want him to kiss me right now.

But instead he says, "Naomi never told me what a mutant you were."

Naomi.

That sound you hear is my spirits falling to earth.

"Where'd she go, anyway?" I ask.

"I actually don't know." He seems annoyed when he says it—hurt, even. But then he covers it with "I can't say I minded. I'd much rather be here with you."

I don't know why, but I find myself asking, "Is that really true?"

Ely shakes his head. "Man, I can only imagine what you must think of me."

"Naomi's told me stories," I say.

"I'm sure she has. Were they any good?"

"Not really," I tell him. "I mean, the one with the T.A. serenading you at BBar with 'Don't You Want Me' was kinda funny. The one with the guy who wanted you to write your phone number on his dick with a Sharpie—not so much. And I'm still not entirely sure why that guy gave you the maple syrup. I guess the truth is, I like you better in person."

"That's funny. I've always liked Naomi's version of me the best. I'm always much more interesting when she talks about me."

"Well, maybe you're mistaken," I say.

And he looks me in the eye and says, "Well, maybe I am."

The two of us are just sitting there. And it's not as if the air is charged with sexual electricity. But the air isn't empty, either. It's just a . . . normal moment. We're living in real time.

"And how are *you* a mutant?" I ask.

"Well," he says, "my skull is made of titanium. I have the ability to read minds and part seas. I can make my left arm invisible, if I'm wearing blue. I only need an hour of sleep every night. And I have a third nipple, too."

"Your skull is made of titanium?"

He leans in. "Yeah. Wanna see?"

And it *is* like electricity now. That first shock. Then the amazement that it happened. I touch his hair, his skull underneath. All the fragile non-fragile parts.

Hands in his hair, fingers touching the back of his head, I know this is not love.

But I am afraid—I am amazed—that it could be.

I wish my heart were titanium, too.

MO(U)RNING

So maybe I'm sitting on a bench in Washington Square Park, centered inside the pulse at the heart of the city that doesn't sleep. So maybe it's just me here, and some joggers, a few commuters rushing to their 🚇, the ➘ bums, all of us sharing the view of dawn rising over the Empire State Building and Midtown off in the distance.

But I know the difference. Everyone else is a ghost. I exist here alone, stranded by choice. Deserted.

I'm like Columbus. I discovered this island. It's mine now. I hereby claim sole custody.

Maybe this island bench *used* to be the one where Ely and I would hunker down around dawn, after parties, before going home. Once upon a time, this *was* the bench where he'd place my head in his lap and stroke my hair (or vice versa), where we created our private island for passing the time to let the substances subside before we returned to the nightmare our parents created. In the parallel universe of Naomi & Ely, this *might* be the spot where, if one half of our equation hadn't decided to kiss my boyfriend, Ely would be coaxing me into a sunrise nap at this very moment, protectively placing a blanket over my body and snarling at any dude who dared ogle me with preying eyes. (Of course, I'd offer up the same Fuck Off glare to all the gay boys returning home from their late-night clubbing who'd dare offer up a smile Ely's way. I give great snarl. I'm not entirely without talent.)

(Maybe Ely didn't snarl at the men ogling me. Maybe I only wanted him to.)

Is this what divorce feels like—complete failure? Dad may have moved out over a year ago, but only now do I understand why, still, the only time Mom wants to get out of bed is when she has to. She's yet to file the official papers, but the word— *divorce*—creeps and crawls, taunts, all over the marital bed where she's taken refuge. Mom knows the other words— *adultery, separation*—found their way to her bed. *Divorce* will, too, when it's ready.

I'll take bench over bed. Still.

On weekends when we were in high school, while all hell broke loose between our parents, Ely and I would take refuge in his room and play a game of Turn Back the Clock. We imagined the late '90s, before all hell broke loose in New York City and the rest of the world, to be a good era to re-invent, so we'd pass lazy Sundays on his bed, listening to early Britney, middle Spice Girls, and late Lilith Fair chicks, or watching DVDs of TV shows that used to air on the former teen angst WB network. I loved to nap on his pillows because they smelled like him, like comfort and boy.

Ely and Bruce the Second are probably wrapped in each other in Ely's bed together right now. It's only been a few days, but Ely doesn't waste time when he's on the hunt—especially if there's potential to score a convert over to his team. What challenge! What fun! No time for mourning this morning! Not when Ely's probably at this very moment laughing and kissing with Bruce the Dead to Me, oblivious that their *their* is like a gun to my head.

The ⚷ underneath my apartment's doormat, Ely's key, has been removed. The monsters under my bed will have to find someone else to scare them away. Ely's services shall no longer be required. I don't need my bed anyway. I've got a bench to sit on. Catatonic. Take *that*, monsters. I will never again lie in my bed alone at night, wishing for Ely.

I feel for Mom, but I'm not going to be her, stranded on the isle of denial. I'm not.

I can't lie. My deserted island isn't populated entirely by me and ghosts. An archangel lingers nearby.

Here's what I want to know: He works graveyard hours as a doorman, plays basketball before his shift, and occasionally performs with his band in Alphabet City in the dead of night when his shift ends early . . . so when exactly *does* Gabriel sleep?

If I was Gabriel and it was seven in the morning and I'd just gotten off work after one of my shifts that did not close out in Alphabet City, I would not be sitting on a park bench, hiding my face under a baseball hat, pretending to be immersed in a book. I would be zzzzzzzzzzzz. I would at least be curled up next to my mom, ready to zzzzzzzzzzzz. Which I plan to be as soon as I can haul ass over to the Starbucks off Waverly Place so I can return home with morning caffeine for her.

First I have to know why Gabriel is playing with me.

I know he knows I'm sitting only a few benches away. I know he's sitting there because I'm sitting here. I know he must be confused that I showed up at his band's show and then had nothing to say to him after. Does he know I left the club and stayed over at girl-Robin's because apparently I hadn't finished the crying I'd started earlier that night at her dorm? I wanted to stay and hang out with him, but more than that, I wanted to turn back time on the end-of-the-world fight with Ely.

I for sure know Gabriel is not actually reading *Message in a Bottle*. I do know someone needs to salvage Gabriel out of late-night poker games with Bruce the First.

I should stand up, go over to him, break the ice with him finally. Engage.

Ely and I *used* to have a No Kiss List™.

Gabriel is a free agent now. I not only could kiss him, I could go much, much farther with him. I could make real Ely's fantasies about Gabriel, in ways that Ely never stood a chance.

As far as I recall, Ely and I never created a No Fuck List?

(Should we have?)

All bets are off now, right?

Mom says men can't be trusted.

I can't.

I should.

Gabriel has big ears.

I don't.

I remain alone on my 🏝️. I have nothing to 🗣️.

But so much to brood over on my deserted-island bench. Now that Ely has eradicated himself as my best friend, my soulmate, the truth is I'm going to have to figure out what to do with my time. School is a waste. Maybe I'll find religion. I'll probably become a ✡. They have the best food.

Gabriel must hear my rumbling stomach over on his island. He makes the first move, signaling my island with a text message to my cell phone.

Can I buy u breakfast?

Sometimes giant pieces of ice, like almost the size of cities, detach from glaciers. They float iceberg majesty—or terror, if you're on the *Titanic*.

I'm sure to go down for this, but I do it anyway. I text back:

Aren't u supposed 2 ask me that the night b4, not the morning of?

The man under the baseball hat doesn't look up. But I see his fingers tap away.

A gentleman shows more respect 2 a lady.

I'm bored. This is pointless. I have nothing left.

If I wasn't a lady, I might be the ~~Bruce~~ laughing and kissing in bed with Ely this morning.

I don't answer.

Yet the gorgeous big-eared man under the Mets hat will not back down.

C'mon. Eggs. Bacon. Home fries. My treat.

I really am kind of hungry. I give:

I like cereal. I leave out the "with Ely" part. My fingers hurt too much to key those additional letters.

The archangel wants to know:

What kind?

I lie:

Product 19.

Truthfully, I like Rice Krispies, with Ely across the breakfast table (at his apartment), eating Lucky Charms. We play food-fight war: Snap! Crackle! Pop! vs. pink hearts, yellow moons, orange stars, and green clovers. Chaos prevails. Ginny throws a fit over the mess. Susan laughs and tosses Grape-Nuts like confetti.

Gabriel tosses back:

I'm a Müeslix man myself.

I'll bet Gabriel knows who Fred Astaire's favorite dance partner was, too.

Seriously? I have to ask.

I see the shape of his fine, fine form laughing from yonder island.

No. Just making sure ur paying attention. I'm all about the Cheerios.

Cheerios are Ely's backup favorite morning cereal, after we've eaten up the Lucky Charms (dry) in the afternoons.

My body aches, my soul grieves. The smile that wants to taunt my lips: DENIED DENIED DENIED. I am not going to be the girl with the heart of stone waiting to be broken down by the quirky-cool guy with the heart of gold. Fuck that fantasy formula.

Persnickety. That's what Ely would text me now, his favorite word to tease and taunt away my dark moods. *Quit it. B Angel Naomi, I no u can.*

I want to be touched by an angel.

His name was Ely, not Gabriel.

My heart is ϴ.

I'd rather have breakfast with Mom.

I text a final message to Gabriel:

I feel sick. Going home.

Ely never wakes up before eight. If I get home soon, we can avoid face time entirely. We're already not speaking—no worries there.

Still. A custody arrangement needs to be worked out. Who gets to use the elevator, the laundry room, the lobby—when. Separate but equal. Dead to one another.

There will be no ☞ this time.

WEEKIVERSARY

I know things are really getting twisted when I think to myself that it would be better if she were dead. Like, then I could have all these good memories and be really sad and everyone would understand and eventually I'd move on, cherishing her always. I wouldn't have to do anything about it, because it would be irrevocable. There's something appealing about that.

But of course I don't really want her dead. I'm glad she's alive. It's all the good memories that are dead.

Dumped doesn't even begin to describe it. If you're going to use a trash metaphor, *incinerated* is more like it.

I don't know if she wants me dead, but she's made it pretty clear that she doesn't want me to exist.

Thou shalt not use the laundry room on Saturdays.

Thou shalt look through your peephole and make sure I am not in the foyer when you're going to the elevator.

Thou shalt go and check your mail if you see me waiting for the elevator in the lobby.

Thou shalt go straight to the elevator if you see me checking my mail.

Thou shalt avoid the following Starbucks: Astor Place (the one on the triangle, not the one close to St. Marks), Broadway between Bowery and Houston, University between Eighth and Ninth.

And so on. Only she didn't phrase them like this. Instead it was:

Don't use the laundry room on Saturdays.

Look through your peephole and make sure I'm not in the foyer when you're going to the elevator. I'll do the same.

Check your mail if you see me waiting for the elevator in the lobby; go straight to the elevator if you see me checking my mail. I'll do the same.

Here are the Starbucks I'd like to go to; please go to other ones.

She had Bruce the First deliver the commandments to me, and even he looked a little embarrassed. I didn't show them to Bruce the Second, because I knew they would only make him feel guilty and sad. He feels guilty and sad enough already.

I'm stuck on incomprehension. I don't understand why she's doing this. I don't understand how something that's held strong for so long could crumble so fast. I mean, not over a boy.

I called. I did. The next morning. That afternoon. Then the day after that.

I thought we needed to cool down, and then we'd be back to being us again.

Instead: incinerated.

I wasn't going to lie and say I was sorry; there wasn't any

reason for me to say I was sorry, except for the Bruce the Second thing, but I was pretty sure this wasn't about the Bruce the Second thing. And the joke was—it's not like Bruce and I were suddenly condom companions. No, that first night, all the clothes stayed on. And when we went to sleep— I don't know how to describe it. It felt like someone had left a night-light on. It had that small glow.

Now it's been a week—and, to be honest, if I were to treat it like an anniversary, I'd say it's the weekiversary of Naomi & Ely's incineration, not Bruce & Ely's relationship. I've never been one to take it slow—I mean, why wait?—but I think because Naomi and I are crashing so fast, Bruce and I are taking it slow. Like, nursing-home slow. Doing the things that end with -alking instead of the ones that end with -ucking.

I'm being careful with him, even if I don't know why. I guess I just sense that I should.

He hasn't asked me back to his dorm, and I'm not sure whether that's because he doesn't want people to know he's with a guy or if he just doesn't want them to know he's with me. I don't really mind. My bed's more comfortable than anything NYU provides anyway—I've had a good sampling. Naomi was always more into dorm beds than I was.

We go for dinner at Chat 'n Chew and a movie at Union Square. Then it's almost midnight and he has a morning class, so we decide to call it a night. In front of his dorm, there's that sweet moment when he so clearly wants me to kiss him good-bye and he's clearly still too nervous to kiss me good-bye, so I lean into him and we kiss right there. It's brief, because Bruce is still so shy, and it's not like kissing in public with other guys, where it's all about showing off or showing each other. With Bruce, it's about the kiss itself. I don't know how he does that. I mean, I don't know how he does that *to me*.

I'll admit that I still don't get it. As I'm walking home, I'm as much amused as I am aroused. Then I get into our lobby and all the blissful feelings are drained away, leaving me with my hurt and resentment and anger. Even if Naomi wasn't there, I'd feel these things, just from the way she's turned my home against me, the way she's haunted it with all her damage. But because Naomi *is* there, I'm almost paralyzed with the hurt and resentment and anger I feel.

She's checking her mail. I know what the rule is. I know I am to head directly to the elevator.

But I never agreed to the rule. I was never even asked.

I nod to Gabriel as I pass him, but he's too caught up in a book to notice. Then I take out my mail key and head into the small mailroom.

I've only taken a step inside when she asks, "What are you doing?" She doesn't even turn around to say it. Just looks at her mailbox. Glares.

"I'm checking my mail," I say lightly.

She slams her mailbox shut. Locks it. Faces me. Says, "Fuck you."

"Sorry," I say, pointing to an imaginary ring on my wedding finger. "Already taken."

I know it's a bitchy response, but where I come from, "Fuck you" does not require a polite response.

"I told you not to do this," she says.

"No," I correct, "you didn't *tell* me anything. Telling requires actual *vocal contact*. You *wrote a list* that said I shouldn't do this. Which is, I might add, majorly childish—and not the good kind of childish, either."

I have seen her this unhappy before. Never about a boy. Not about that. But about her mom and my mom, and about her dad leaving, and about her grandfather dying. All of those sadnesses held a different degree of anger. This one—right now—is near the top of the scale.

"C'mon, Naomi," I say. "This is so silly."

"Yeah, it's a total barrel of laughs."

"That's not what I meant."

" 'Silly.' "

"Look—"

"No, *you* look," she interrupts. "You blew it. You *totally* blew it. You had me—you really had me—buying into this whole Cult of Ely that you created. But you know what? I've turned in my membership card. I'm getting my own life, because I'm sick and tired of sharing one with you. You're not good for me, Ely. You've shot me down one too many times. I'm tattooing you at the top of my No Kiss List."

"I should've *always* been tattooed at the top of your No Kiss List! I mean, *duh*!" I can't believe this. "It's not about kissing, Naomi. Give me a break."

"Oh, I'll give you a break. A clean one. I've put up with your shit and your drama and your carelessness for so goddamn long. *How dare you.* You come in here, having just fucked my boyfriend of a week ago, pretending to get your mail when you and I both know that Ginny picks up the mail every day when she gets home from work, and you make it seem like this is all *my* fault. 'Fuck you' isn't big enough for that, Ely. And, to top it all off, you're wearing my goddamn jeans!"

This is definitely incineration, because I'm feeling hot and burned and fierce and intense.

"You want your jeans back?" I shout. "Well, here." I kick off my shoes, one of them hitting the lowest row of mailboxes. I take off my belt. Rip open the button fly and pull off the jeans. Then I ball them up and throw them right at her. "You happy?" I ask her. "Is that what you wanted?" I am crying now, this is so wrong. I am crying, because I don't want this to be happening and still it's happening and it even feels like it has to happen, but I'm so sad and angry and resentful and hurt and Naomi just looks shocked. She throws the jeans to the ground and calls me an asshole and just leaves me there, crying in my boxers, the biggest fucking fool, the angriest bewildered object of incineration, and there's nothing to do but wait until I hear the elevator arrive, wait until I hear it leave, wait enough time for her to get upstairs, for her to get inside, then take the same exact route, only too far behind for any of it to matter. I think about leaving the jeans outside her door, then I think about taking them back with me, and ultimately, I just take them to the garbage chute and throw them down. Neither of us will wear them now. It's best if they're done.

Incinerated.

BINGO

Divide and conquer has been both a successful military strategy and an algorithm design paradigm. Military leaders theorized that it would be easier to defeat one army of 50,000 men followed by another army of 50,000 men than to conquer a single 100,000-man unit. Combat would be best served by dividing the enemy into two forces and then conquering one followed by the other. As an algorithm design technique, the divide-and-conquer principle requires dividing the problem into two smaller subproblems, solving each of them recursively, and then melding the two partial solutions into one solution to the full problem. When the merging takes less time than solving the two subproblems, an efficient algorithm results.

Naomi and Ely are probably both too self-absorbed to notice, but they seem to be going for the military version of *divide and conquer* within our building, although I doubt either of them is intelligent enough to understand the mathematical paradigm. *I* barely do, and I scored ninety-eighth percentile on the math PSAT.

The long-awaited Naomi-Ely meltdown finally happened in our building lobby, but it's taken time for word to get around. Not *everyone* hangs out in the lobby in the middle of the night. Some of us actually sleep at night. So it's only now becoming clear, based on the division of bingo seating, where loyalties in the building are divided. It still remains to be seen who shall be conquered—and who shall be the conqueror.

From viewing tonight's bingo seating in the building's basement-level multi-purpose room, loyalties appear to be split straight down the middle, like the groom's side and bride's side at a wedding. To the left we have among the Naomi contingent: the illegal subletter in 15B; Bruce, my twin brother and not the new boyfriend of Ely; Mr. McAllister, who will always sway to the side of the better-endowed mammary glands; Naomi's mom's friends from the co-op board, who sided with her mom during the time of the bitter breakup feud between 15J and 15K; the residents of floor fourteen, who all agree that Naomi and her mom make less upstairs floor noise than Ely and his moms; and me. But I'm a variable coefficient, sitting here only to protect my brother from her. Again. To the right, the Ely contingent includes: PFLAG members from assorted floors; That Other Bruce, who, for a guy outfitted by the Gap, really has a lot of unexpected nerve showing up here tonight; every gentleman in the building who ever shared hot looks in the elevator with Naomi only to have their advances rebuffed (why did my brother have to be the exception? *Oy!*); and the

Lesbian Nation of Ginny and Susan and all their comrades with the bad Park Slope haircuts.

I've created a monster. I only started the bingo nights at my building to fulfill my high school community service requirement. I figured we'd get ten residents max, all over the age of seventy, we'd meet for games like five times and then like forget all about it, and I'd get my school credit and be done with it. But noooooo. Everyone wanted in on bingo—everyone from the building, the block, the borough. I didn't count on that variable, and now it's, like, out of control with hipsters here. Whatever happened to billiards as the hot group game of choice? People, I'm trying to get into Harvard here—not start a revolution!

Che, I mean She who leads us, is she who shall not be conquered—our resident bingo caller, Mrs. Loy, who cares only about bingo and not at all about the Naomi-Ely-Bruce1-Bruce2 quadrangle. Mrs. Loy is loyal only to her dog and to my brother, who treats her dog more like a sister than he does his own sister, she who happens to be me. Back in nineteen hundred forever ago, long before she moved to Manhattan to marry old what's-his-name, Mrs. Loy once competed in the U.K. Caller of the Year Competition, which is like this big-deal contest where bingo callers compete for a cash prize and the chance to call the numbers in Las Vegas, as well as to become the bingo "ambassador" for Britain. Mrs. Loy didn't win, but she seems more than happy to settle for serving as our building's bingo ambassador so many years later.

"Dirty Gertie!" she calls out. The only way to thin out the ranks of our game's burgeoning popularity was to require players to learn U.K. Housie slang. Room occupancy deference to fire department hazard codes.

"What number is 'Dirty Gertie'?" Bruce my twin brother asks me. Thirty-fifth percentile on the PSAT. His mathematical experiment was to choose "All of the above" as the answer to every fourth problem. Boy needs to get a good night's sleep. Otherwise, he'll be lucky to get accepted at SUNY–So Far Upstate You Might As Well Be In Canada, *eh?*

I cross out the number 30 on his card. I have to do everything for him. I'm five minutes older. The burden always falls on me.

Mrs. Loy spots me in the crowd and I know what number will be called out next. I cross out the number 1 on my card well before she calls out, "Kelly's Eye!"

Next up is "Two Fat Ladies!" and I would so have bingo if number 88 was on my card. I avoid looking directly up at Amstel Not-So-Light Susan and Ginny, because that would be too obvious. They're not really fat, even, they're more just . . . relaxed, not heterosexually emaciated, like most of the other building moms, e.g., my mom, Naomi's mom. I'm glad they worked things out, although my parents voted against them in the co-op board dispute, because Mom and Dad wanted to buy the moms' apartment, directly downstairs from ours, and break through to build us a bi-level apartment. So I'm sort of grateful to the moms as well, since I really could not get behind my mother's menopausal plan to adopt a contingent of special-needs babies from Macedonia once Bruce and I take off for college. My mom breaks down in sobs when salesclerks at Bendel don't recognize her. I don't think she could handle the pressure.

"Heinz Varieties!" That Other Bruce across the room is close. I can feel it. He just crossed out number 57 on his card. How a guy that bland and nice got caught up in the Naomi & Ely situation beats me. I mean, Ely's hot, but not *that* hot—except when he's paying me top dollar for my Gremlin aka Titanium Man's appearance in vintage *X-Men vs. The Avengers* #1.

If That Other Bruce reaches bingo before me, I will not be happy. I wonder if he's miserable when he's trapped in the elevator with Naomi and Ely at the same time. The freeze is so cold between Naomi and Ely, both Iceman and Emma Frost are shivering from their silence.

My Bruce points at my recently delivered burger and fries container. Food is strictly forbidden on the bingo tables, but since I am not only the master of this game but also fix most every resident here's computer when it breaks down and consequently know all the sordid details of their online porn, gambling, and illegal music-downloading addictions, nobody dares call me out on my rule bending.

"Are you going to eat your fries?" Bruce asks me.

"No."

"Can I have some, then?"

"No." I push the container farther out of his reach.

Mrs. Loy calls out, "Man Alive!"

My stupid brother's fry distraction causes That Other Bruce to beat me at finding the number 5 on my card. "Bingo!" he calls out. Now I'm furious. That Other Bruce is joyful. He waves his card in the air, smiling. He turns to Ely and they share a quick, celebratory kiss. Not the lip-to-lip kind, or the tongue kind—it's only a quick cheek kiss, but still, that does it for Naomi. I bet it hurts way more for your ex–best friend to steal your boyfriend and then have their thing turn out to potentially be true love than just to lose the friend and the boyfriend to a casual fling. I'd feel sorry for her if she wasn't such a bitch about manipulating my brother because of it. Right now Naomi looks like she'd want to throw herself into Terrigen Mist, which for those not properly schooled in the Marvel universe is a mutagenic, or mutation-causing, substance discovered by the Inhuman scientist Randac. It is potent enough to cause any living organism to mutate from exposure to it.

Naomi responds to the kiss by purposefully, scarily, turning to my Bruce. She places her hand at the back of his neck to pull him back in, and *BAM*, once again my brother has forgotten all about our parents' lectures on safe sex *and* disgusting PDAs. Ewww... I should have given him my fries; maybe that would have kept his mouth too tied up for his and Naomi's lip-to-lip, tongue-swirling display.

That's it. I've had it. I've lost a bingo round I was *thisclose* to winning *and* my brother has publicly revolted me for the last time. Mr. McAllister is handing out new cards, but I'll sacrifice the next round to end this nonsense contest once and for all.

"NAOMI!" I say.

She's already forgotten my brother as she detaches her mouth from his and leans in front of him to reach for a fry from my container. "What is it, Kelly?" she asks, dipping the fry into the ketchup before taking a bite.

Bruce is sitting right between us, but I speak to her as if he's not there. I think even in the womb, I knew this was the best method for dealing with him—by going around him. And if his post-contact-with-Naomi crotch pops one up in full view of me, he is banned from this game and from my protection from this day forward. Boys are so . . . so . . . *useless.*

"Naomi," I say. "How would *you* feel if someone you liked teased you into thinking you had a relationship you in fact don't have?"

I understand that I should be more tactful with my words, but clearly I'm not the only person concerned with Naomi's behavior. Everyone at our table stops paying attention to Mrs. Loy long enough to see Naomi's reaction. Naomi is a powder keg waiting to blow, a Rogue waiting to happen, and no one wants to miss the explosive transformation. She's so . . . so . . . *ripe.*

Naomi actually thinks about my question. I give her credit. She looks over to Ely and That Other Bruce, who are now intently staring at their game cards so no one would dare think they cared about observing Naomi's make-out moment with my brother. Ewww, again.

"You're right," Naomi states. It's spooky how beautiful she is—it's like her hazel eyes have gotten deeper and more alluring from all the crying they've obviously experienced lately. All eyes are on her beauty as she stands up from our table. She's wearing low (*very* low)-rider jeans with a tight (*very* tight) T-shirt that says THE ABE FROMAN EXPERIENCE on it, and her exposed belly exposes a new belly ring that has the elevator rejects on the Ely side of the game room salivating from the view of it. She looks down at my seated Bruce. "You know I love you, right? But not the way you'll ever want me to. And the temptress routine can get tiring, and I am all-out exhausted these days. So get over me, okay, Bruce? Move on. And, Kelly, I owe you thanks for setting Bruce and me free from recycling this game over and over. You're a good girl and I hope you get into Harvard one day, I sincerely do. Because I sincerely know what you're talking about, and the answer is, it feels like shit, and I shouldn't be causing someone else to feel that."

I can't believe that lying wench is capable of such sincere compassion. I don't think she's messing with us, either. I think she actually had a revelatory moment, and I think I actually inspired it. I think her hurt has inspired a new direction. Maybe a better one.

Trust Ely to tip the moment, of course. *That* wench can't just let Naomi's rare moment of decency go by without ruining it. He turns to Bruce the Other and plants one on *his* lips, a deep one this time. Even the Lesbian Nation appears mortified. Bruce the Other looks like he wants to die from the public display. I heard he wasn't even gay 'til Ely. Trust Ely to take the moment too far, and to push his new boyfriend too soon—

not just out of the closet, but too far out into the happily happening world of West Ninth Street bingo.

Naomi says, "I get it now. Ely was the lie." Then she very loudly proclaims, looking up at the ceiling like she's calling out to God, but Lord have mercy, it's not like every bingo player in the room doesn't understand exactly to which he her words are directed: "AND THE STARBUCKS ON SIXTH BY WAVERLY IS MINE!"

And having so spoketh, Naomi runs out of the room. Through the clear window on the community room door, I see Gabriel standing outside. Waiting to comfort her. Now there's a situation that could be *way* more scandalous than the Naomi and Ely breakup.

I fear for Naomi's new quest for truth as much as I hated her old quest to conquer my brother.

REALIZE

It can't last longer than a minute. I just have to ▣ the room, walk out the door. But it's like I've suddenly overdosed on Saint-John's-wort. Because while it's not unusual for me to have twenty-seven thoughts at once, it's definitely unusual to be hearing every single one of them pass through my mind in the time it takes for me to leave a room.

① Walk. Just. Keep. Walking. Don't look at anyone. Don't look at the ground. Focus. Straight. Ahead. Just. Keep. Walk-ing.

② Okay, you *pussy-teasing faggot,* do you know what I'm going to do to you? I am going to take back that boy whose lips you are currently fellating, and I am going to ▣ you pictures of him doing things to me that he'd never, ever be able to do to your ♦. Every time you step out of the elevator, I'm going to make sure that he and I are jammed together on the other side of the wall, releasing moans that are going to make you *scramble* to find some porn. I will take him by the ⬇ and lead him away from you, and I will make you watch every. fucking. moment.

③ This is too much. This is too far. This isn't really happening.

④ I showed you mine and you showed me yours. Kindergarten. Maybe first grade. Mom was in the other room, watching her soaps (before our lives became one). You had to pee and I went in to watch you. It was curiosity. That one place where we were different. Only that one place. Otherwise, we assured each other, we were completely the same.

⑤ Are you happy now, Kelly? Did you get what you wanted? ✝, I can't stand you. I hope you get into your poison Ivy League school and disappear into a physics lab and never return.

⑥ It's the shoes. If I hadn't chosen these shoes this morning, none of this would have happened. The pumps are to blame.

⑦ I kissed Bruce first. People are forgetting that. I kissed him first. That has to give me some kind of right, even if he ends up being gay.

⑧ I have printed out every e-mail you ever sent me. And that horrible year, when Mom would disappear and Dad would fume and cry and yell, all I could do when you weren't home was go to my room and take out the box and read something stupid about the velour pantsuit that Mrs. Keller wore to school that day, and how you thought it made her look like Barney's bastard love child, and I would find myself smiling, because even though the 🌐 was falling apart and our parents had turned our lives into a ☂, I honestly believed that you were the only family I needed. My future family.

⑨ One spot. I was just one spot away from bingo.

⑩⓿ *B-I-N-G-O. B-I-N-G-O. B-I-N-G-O. And Bingo was his name-O.* What I want to know is: What the fuck does the 🐕 have to do with the game? There has to be some connection, right?

⑩① Did I really just dump Bruce the First, the one person in this whole city who worships the ground I stalk on? So what if he's a ✂. Isn't it enough to have someone who adores you even when you're not being adorable? Isn't it enough to love someone because you know he's going to be nice to you? Does there really have to be a sexual charge? Isn't it enough to feel it in your ♥ even if you're not feeling it ⬇?

⑩② Who the fuck am I kidding?

⑩③ I'm not kidding myself, that's for sure.

①④ Robin (♀) has the right idea. When Robin (♂) told her he just wanted to be friends, she threw her ♈ at him. Just picked up her appletini and splashed it over his just-wanna-be-friends expression. Then she stormed out and left him to pay for the drink she'd just emptied onto his face. I think it's the last part I admire the most. (Of course, afterward she cried for about six days, which was about five and a half more than I could really stomach. I told her the only person a ♂ named Robin should date is a guy named Batman, so they can live in their Brokeback Batcave and ♋. I told her she could do better, even though she probably can't. That's what friends are for.)

①⑤ I miss Dad. Even when all of these other things are going on, even when he should be two thousand miles away from my thoughts, I wish he was here. Not so we could return to the fighting time, but back farther than that, to the good time. I know he and Mom both say now that the good time wasn't really that good, but what matters to me is that I didn't know it then. I felt it was good, and even though that's selfish, it's really good enough for me.

①⑥ Do you remember, Ely, the way we'd always be picking places to get married? How many years did we do that? In front of the polar bear pool at the Central Park Zoo. Or in a swank soirée at the Temple of Dendur. Or on the Staten Island Ferry, with the guests changing every time we docked. Or at the top of the Empire State Building, before we realized how cliché that was. Then just this August, when you dragged me to XXL so you could flirt with one of the go-go boys while all the gone-gone boys hit on me . . . at one point between oglings, you leaned over to me and said, "Maybe we should get married *here*." And I laughed, because it was funny. And I was happy that you'd made us into an us again, in a place that wouldn't treat us like an us. And I was upset—really upset— that you weren't taking it seriously, that you would never take it seriously. Even though it was ridiculous, I wanted you to care.

①⑦ I am so over guys. Even gay guys. Especially gay guys. Sympathize all you want, boys, but when it all comes down to it, you still have dicks.

①⑧ Look, there's Gabriel. He's looking very, very gazeworthy tonight.

①⑨ Oh, Mrs. Loy, don't glare at me like I'm a strumpet. I know you want Bruce the First to be the Harold to your Maude, and now you should be royally pleased that I'm freeing him from the shackles of being sadly in love with me. Maybe he'd like a real Dame for a change.

②⓪ It shouldn't be called a multi-purpose room. It's a no-purpose room.

②① Almost there. Almost there.

②② I'm so glad I didn't sleep with Bruce the First. And by *sleep with,* I mean *have intercourse with.* We did a lot of sleeping, and that was nice. In fact, 📟 was the nicest part. I'm glad I'm smart enough to know that not getting to have intercourse with your first choice for your first is not reason enough to have intercourse with choice #2.

②③ I'm so tired. Tired of the drama. Tired of missing Ely. Tired of spending all my time trying not to miss him. Tired of being so fucking angry. At him. At Mom. At Dad. And most of all at the universe. Tired of having to deal with people. Tired of not getting anything close to what I want. Tired of having the wrong people want me. Tired of wanting the wrong people. Tired of the 💬 and the 🎈 and the 🗯. Tired of thinking. Tired of the games. But if I got rid of all of that—what would I have left?

②④ Why is Gabriel smiling like that? It's like he knows the ⊜List™ has been ✂ into pieces.

②⑤ Danger! Danger!

②⑥ Do you really have anything left to lose?

②⑦ Go for it.

TRACKS

Track 1
Chris Isaak: "Graduation Day"

This is the song for both of us: the past.

The day we met was your graduation day—yours and Ely's. Make that *night*. It was night. You and Ely still wore your graduation robes. You were both ripped. The parties were long over, but the two of you cuddled on the lobby sofa until dawn, empty champagne bottles at your feet. You laughed and sang songs. You seemed to be making up ditties on the spot as you goaded one another into belches. That was your game, seeing who could push the other the farthest.

Your graduation day was my first night on the job. I wondered why the building residents who passed through the lobby took no notice of you and Ely—like that's how you could be found on any night, two drunken teenagers wearing graduation robes, burping and singing and teasing, holding on to one another for dear life and yet not groping one another, either. Whispering secrets.

Look, it's no secret that I've turned out to be a lousy doorman. Everyone in the building knows it. The benefit of working a graveyard shift is that very few residents are awake enough to be bothered by my incompetence. So I misplace packages, and I mispronounce residents' names. *You* try saying, "Nope, there's no DHL, UPS, or FedEx for you here, Mr. Dziechciowski," at four in the morning. So I buzz the wrong apartments and send food-delivery guys upstairs to bring steak sandwiches to the Singhs or BLTs to the Lefkowitzes . . . before dawn on a Saturday morning. Sorry. And don't forget the middle-of-the-night rotation of visitors dealing dope or adultery who I let slide by. Just don't ask me to gossip about all the goings-on with the congregation of lobby insomniacs. Because I don't care. I'm just gonna stand at the doorman station lookin' cool. That, I do well.

I'm a nineteen-year-old guy with nothing better to do than moonlight as a doorman, and daydream about you.

I thought you loved me / I was wrong. Life goes on.

Sorry, that line refers to another girl, who's not you. My life has gone on without her.

You couldn't know the imprint you left on me that first night, how I'd arrived on the job feeling like it was the first day of the end of my life. You couldn't know what had recently been buried, or left behind. You couldn't know that the simple sight of your dimpled smile at me that night, and the sound of your laughter, gave me the smallest glimmer of hope when all I wanted to do was bolt—from the new job, from home—to go anywhere or nowhere, to disappear into nothing.

Even the smallest glimmer counts.

Track 2
Bettye Swann: "(My Heart Is) Closed for the Season"

This song is for Lisa.

Let's get this out of the way now. Lisa was my first. I got piercings in private places for her. Combat boots and a nurse's uniform, that was Lisa. A goth hospice nurse—go figure. Ah, figure. Voluptuous, a smart-ass with a smart ass. Who could resist?

Let's also get this out of the way now. Slap any sexual or ethnic label on me that you want, but don't—I repeat, don't— label me on the basis of my musical tastes. My dad claims he learned to speak English from listening to country music; my mother believed music was how we should communicate as a family. My parents used to trap my brother and me into helping them with weekend home-improvement projects under the guise of our "musical education." We were hostages to Dad's love of vinyl honky-tonk and funk, and Mom's fondness for sad soul singers and Clash-era Brits. Because of my parents' alluring baits of grilled cheese sandwiches and endless air hockey games as rewards for time lost to tiling kitchens and bathrooms, I'm a sucker for Hank Williams (Sr.) and old-school girl soul singers from the non-Motown pack.

Okay, so admittedly I first heard this song on a Starbucks compilation, but it wouldn't be right to hold that against the song. It's not the song's fault.

The Lisa-ness of this particular oldie girl's timeless song message? Seasons change. Closure and transition. Whatever. We'll address The Obviousness of Irony in later song selections.

Lisa was older. I guess you figured that by now. She wasn't Mrs. Loy old, the kind of old that defies actual numbers. Lisa was of an age that she'd been around long enough to get married and divorced, to know where piercings should be situated for maximum effect.

My brother said I had displaced attachment. Like if I loved her nurse, then that love could somehow keep our mother alive.

Lisa left me a week after. She said she'd been meaning to break up with me for a month, but I was too vulnerable. So she waited until after the funeral.

All I can do is lock up my heart and get over you.

Go to college, Lisa said. Join a band. Act your age. Enjoy it.

I joined a band just so I could call her and tell her I joined it. Do you even know who Abe Froman is? she asked me. I said no. She said that was exactly why we could no longer be together. Generation gap. Act your age, she repeated. Find someone your own age.

I'm in a band, I can hook the girls in if I want to. I'm like you. I've got the right looks, if you know what I mean. And I don't mean that in a vain way. Just being honest.

Honestly, I'd rather do a lot of things than be a doorman or perform with a band that switches identities from screamo acid jazz to indie-breed melancholy merely to accommodate whatever dive club will let them play. I just haven't figured out what those other things I'd like to do are yet.

Honestly or foolishly (is there a difference?), I can't be bothered to hook up with girls girls girls. I'm a disgrace to my looks and to my age. Five girls asked me to my high school prom last year, and I chose to play cards that night with Lisa, on a bench outside Mom's room. I'm like my dad. I can focus on only one woman at a time—and I want her to be forever and for always.

You're the first since my first to make me feel something, anything. I don't exactly know why—I hardly know you. Maybe I suspect you're like me. If you ever gave the matter substantial thought (and I hope you have), I suspect you'd also recognize that the Temptations were bound to factory hit-songwriting, and that's why they got it wrong. Beauty's *not* only skin deep. Just because a person is beautiful doesn't mean there's no soul beneath. Doesn't mean that person hasn't suffered like everyone else, doesn't mean they don't hope to still be a good human being in an awful world.

Hope. That's what you make me feel.

That smallest glimmer could expand.

Track 3
Belle & Sebastian: "Piazza, New York Catcher"

This song is for you and Ely.

You and Ely hummed this song to one another when you passed me by my first weeks on the job. You didn't think I got it, but I understood the underlying message. *Gabriel, night-time doorman, are you straight or are you gay?*

Like it's not enough that people look at me and wonder, *Is he brown or yellow or white or what?*

As I mentioned, aside from my musical taste, I don't care what anyone wants to label me, but for the record? Father from the lighter side of the dark continent, mother from the land of the midnight sun via the land of the rising sun. Straight.

Was I mean or kind or neither for letting Ely flirt with me those long summer weeks when you were in Kansas visiting your dying grandfather? Hanging out with Ely in the middle of the night was like a cheating way to get to know you before I was ready to do the work. When Ely talked about you, about the lives you'd shared growing up together, I pictured the two of you as some she-male Eloise at the Plaza, knowing every dark passageway, every nuance of every resident, every secret. I wanted to scavenge your heart through his memories.

I wish that you were here with me to pass the dull weekend.

Ely sang this line aloud constantly while you were gone, when he would hover around the doorman station late at night after going out clubbing with his friends. He was singing about you, not me. That much was always clear.

Clearly he wanted to push the boundaries with me. A doorman doesn't get drunkenly accidentally on purpose bumped up against the mailboxes, or called upon to replace a flickering hallway light at three in the morning, and not figure that out. But Ely didn't push further. He never made a move. You should know that.

Do you know why a Scottish band wrote a song about a New York baseball player? I'm concerned. I feel like there's a potential Scottish invasion of the U.S. in the works (England and Wales abstaining). Belle & Sebastian are part of the advance team.

Stay alert.

Track 4
The Jam: "The Bitterest Pill (I Ever Had to Swallow)"

This song is for you and Ely, me and Lisa.

You and I, we both know what it's like to swallow the bitterest brand of pill that people like Ely and Lisa dole out. We understand how it feels to fall prey to the sickness of loving Elys and Lisas—those who won't love you back the way you love them. The pill's bittersweet chaser is not that they *can't* love you back the same way. It's that they *won't*. They won't open their minds to the possibility. They won't expand their expectations of romantic love past their own predetermined boundaries—gender, age, [insert innumerable other unfair, random reasons here].

The love I gave hangs in sad-colored, mocking shadows.
Sucks.

Track 5
Fiona Apple: "Criminal"

This song is for Bruce the First.

Naomi, you've been a bad, bad girl. You've been careless with a delicate ~~man~~ boy.

I don't know you well at all, obviously, but I feel like I could possibly trust you. I have to believe that anyone who lies as much as you do will in the end do the right thing, if for no other reason than you've already stripped bare what's real from what's not. I know you know the difference.

I'm going to trust you not to break that boy just because you can.

Track 6
Nada Surf: "Blizzard of '77"

This song is for my parents.

The first time my father saw snow he was five years old. He had just moved to this country. A blizzard had struck during the night, and when he awoke in the morning, he couldn't see out his bedroom window. Only by sitting on his own father's shoulders could he get a clear view to the vastness of the white outside the front door to their house. The snow was taller than him—my father thought it could swallow him whole if he ventured out into it. Then, as he tells the story, he saw an angel. She was wearing a pink snowsuit, and she sat in her father's lap as they rode a tractor clearing a path from the street to his house. He recognized her from his school class, where no other kid would talk to him because he didn't yet speak English. Once the angel and her father had finished clearing the path, they jumped off the tractor and shoveled the remaining snow leading to his front door. "Welcome, neighbor," she said to him. In Swahili.

My father does not speak Swahili; the Neighborhood Welcome Committee had been misinformed. But he quickly dressed and ventured outside, following the angel's tracks.

He grew up to marry that girl.

Track 7
Kirsty MacColl: "A New England"

This song is for my mother. She loved this singer, and particularly this singer's cover of this Billy Bragg song.

When I dropped off the varsity basketball team in high school, when I neglected to apply to college, when I scorned my brother for his Causes and Ideals, my mother would sing this song, adjusting one lyric in particular because it reminded her of me.

Gabriel doesn't want to change the world / He's not look-ing for a new England.

At the end, when she wanted me to distract her, but really she wanted me to distract myself, Mom asked me to make mixes for her to listen to at the hospital. Just go to the music library on our computer at home, choose some songs, hit shuffle, then burn, she said.

I never made a mix for her that didn't include a Kirsty MacColl song—it's like a law for me now. Any Kirsty Mac-Coll song reminds me of my mom. Whimsical, soulful, funny. Missed.

Both Kirsty MacColl and my mom had two sons. They both died before their forty-fifth birthday.

At least my brother and I knew it was coming. We got to say good-bye.

Track 8
Bruce Springsteen: "It's Hard to Be a Saint in the City"

This is my mother's song for me. Jersey girl.

I was born blue and weathered, but I burst just like a supernova.

What you need is a muse, she used to tell me. A Mary or a Janie. Then she'd say, But be careful. Those Marys and Janies can be dangerous to a boy who could walk like Brando right into the sun and then dance just like a Casanova.

I don't want to be a Brando or a Casanova. I don't even want to be a rock star. Don't know why I'm in a band other than a girl told me to do it. I only front the band because I'm the best-looking of the bunch. The other guys are way more talented.

I wouldn't mind a muse. Or to be amused. That would be a refreshing change.

Track 9
Kurtis Blow: "Basketball"

This is my father's song for me.

Basketbaaaaall, they're playin' basketball, we love that basketball.

For six months after the funeral, Pops laid off me. Day after day, I could be found in the park or at the Y playing pickup b-ball with any team who'd let me hoop. Fine. Dad didn't give me grief about grieving through sweat and dribble, through game.

But man, you never heard such swearing in a language you don't understand as when another year's college application deadlines had passed and I finally told Dad I didn't plan on going back to school—not at all, not ever.

Fine, no more. You think you're going to keep living in my house and spend your days playing basketball? You got no real plans, young man? Well then I got plans for you. You'll be a doorman.

I have to admit that the alternate song choice here was the "Dentist!" song from *Little Shop of Horrors*. If I'd chosen that song, I would have told you to imagine the word *doorman* instead of *dentist* when the guy sings about how Son, you'll be a dentist. I would have explained that the song is about the singer's destiny to become a dentist, as determined by his proclivity for causing people pain, and as decided upon by his parents. The message was meant to be about parents and destiny and not about a desire to be a dentist or to cause pain, by the way.

My father's destiny was to be a doorman. He likes that destiny. It's a fine one, for him. He's worked for decades at the same posh building on Park Avenue. He rakes in the tips at Christmastime. Seriously—our family once vacationed for a week at a four-star resort in Barbados courtesy of that income, before Mom got too sick to travel.

He's a good man and it's been a good life for my dad, being a doorman. I do feel like perhaps it's not my destiny.

I ended up not using the dentist song on your mix, because including a show tune would be too gay even for a guy who doesn't care about labels.

Side note: Do you have any idea what it means when someone says, "That's so gay"? I suspect it has nothing to do with actual homosexuality anymore. I think it means nothing at this point. Really, just nothing. "That's so gay." Totally existential.

Maybe I should have used the dentist song after all.

Track 10
Shuggie Otis: "Inspiration Information"

This song is for the sake of the song.

My dad wants to school me in the noble ways of the Manhattan doorman, but what I've learned from my dad that's actually useful is that you can insert a Shuggie Otis song in any position on any random mix and the song will work. As beginning, as transition, as closure.

And if you have any information regarding inspiration, I'm all ears.

Track 11
Grandmaster Flash: "The Message"

This song is for you.

It's a really depressing song with a great beat and an unforgettable hook. You're kind of a depressing person with a great look and an unforgettable smile—when you choose to flash its grandmasterliness.

It's like a jungle sometimes, it makes me wonder / How I keep from goin' under.

New York City—yeah, it's a jungle. I'll be Tarzan if you want to be Jane. Hell, I'll even be Jane if you want to be Tarzan. My mind is *open,* girl.

Yours could be, too—if you'd let it. You'll let me text-message with you, you'll appear at my band's shows in the middle of the night, but live and in person in the building lobby? You barely have a word to say to me. Like there's some line in the sand between the desk and the doormat that you're too scared to cross.

RU4real?

Track 12
Nina Simone: "Ne Me Quitte Pas"

Cette chanson prend trop de place. (*Merci,* Mr. McAllister, you bilingual freak. You fill up elevator space just like this song does.)

What's the big deal with France? How come everyone wants to go there? Let me tell you about France. Their music sucks. Their movies suck. Their berets suck. Their croissants are pretty good, but the place overall still sucks. My family went there once on the way to visit Dad's homeland family. EuroDisney. Need I say more?

Are you worried that if we have a real conversation, this is the kind of empty chatter that would fill it?

Let's take the risk. Here's a start: If I could choose a place to go, I'd choose . . . random spin of wheel of fortune . . . Madagascar. I feel like it might be one place in the world that's about more than a Starbucks on every block. Want to come along?

Discuss.

Track 13
Jens Lekman: "F-Word"

Jag valde den här sången så at du skule bli förälskad i mej.
I chose this song to make you fall in love with me. (Thank you,
Mr. Karlsson, the unexpected Swede in the penthouse apart-
ment. Or should I say *"tahkk"*?)

Fuck it, here's the stinkin' truth: I'm just trying to be clever
here. I hate myself for choosing a smart-ass song, like it's not
possible to make a mix for a beautiful girl without inserting
some form of obvious ha-ha irony from the Smiths or the
Magnetic Fields, etc. You have to admit it's a cool song, though.
I promise to balance it out with a pathetically sentimental
song choice next.

Track 14
Buffy the Vampire Slayer: "Walk through the Fire"

This song is for you and your mom.

If you took a poll, I'm sorry to tell you that at least 80 percent of the residents in this building who know you or have
come into contact with you would vote Yes, Naomi—she is a
bitch.

Buffy could be a bitch, but cut the girl some slack—she
once had to kill her true love in order to save the world. I get
it, Naomi. You're like Buffy. You have to make hard choices
about people.

Speaking of hardness . . . would you be pleased or weirded out to know Buffy was the girl I used to dream about when, er, getting to know my high school self a little better? Never mind—consider the emission, I mean admission, rescinded.

When your mom noticed me watching a *Buffy* rerun on the little TV on the doorman desk one slow night on the job, she admitted that watching *Buffy* was her shared solace with you after your dad left. She told me how you cry and cry for Buffy. You cry when Angel shows up to be Buffy's prom date even though they'd already recognized the futility of their true love and broken up. You cry when Buffy's mom is taken away by natural instead of supernatural causes. You cry when seasons six and seven really don't reflect the quality of seasons one through five except for the musical episode.

Now through the smoke she calls to me / To make my way across the flame.

Those bitch-calling Naomi naysayers in the building wouldn't know that at six in the morning, when my shift is ending, you rush out of the building and down the block to bring back coffee and bagels for your mom. That you hold her hand and walk her to Washington Square to see her off to work. To make sure she gets there.

Buffy was my mother's solace, too. I'd watch it with her on the good days. My brother would laugh at me and say how gay I was for getting all teary-eyed when Willow went mental after Tara died. Brother-man, love you, but who's laughing now? Who's the doorman / part-time band singer who inspires girls to throw their panties at him on the stage, and who's the impoverished grad student making ends meet by go-go dancing at XXL, where boys slip dollar bills into his G-string?

Track 15
Kylie Minogue: "Come into My World"

This song is for the gays.

Track 16
Elliott Smith: "A Fond Farewell"

This song is for Bruce the Second.

> *I see you're leaving me and taking up with the enemy.*

They really like each other, Naomi. Anyone can see it. They're falling—and it should be a good thing. Let them have it. I volunteer to be the comfort of the in-between.

Track 17
Stevie Wonder: "As"

This song is for Ely.

Naomi, *did* you know that true love asks for nothing?

If you've made it this far on your personalized playlist, you surely now know that while Shuggie Otis works for any track position, Stevie Wonder—not really. Great music, the early stuff—but overpowering to the rest of the set. Do you agree?

But there's a reason for the season. Stevie Wonder. The connection. He ➔ played ➔ piano. According to the tall tales of many longtime building residents, so did you and Ely. Your renditions of "Chopsticks" were legendary.

You offered me a glimmer of hope, so I'm sending some back your way.

I feel confident you and Ely will one day play "Chopsticks" again.

✌

Track 18
Merle Haggard: "Blue Yodel"

This song is for the yodel.

My mom used to say nothing could cure blue moods like a good yodel. She taught me and my brother to yodel with the musical best: Jimmie Rodgers, Don Walser, Merle Haggard.

Go on, try it. *Yo-de-lay-eee-ho.*

Track 19 and Hidden Track 19a
The Ramones: "I Wanna Be Your Boyfriend"

[and]

Prince: "If I Was Your Girlfriend"

This song is for both of us: the future?

The Ramones were greedy with their wannas. They wanna be sedated. They wanna live. They just wanna have something to do tonight. They wanna be your boyfriend.

I'd go for any of those wannas wit' u.

Cuz sometimes I trip on how happy we could be. Please!

OUT

"Why did you do that?" I ask him.

"What?"

He really doesn't know.

"The kiss. Why did you kiss me like that? In front of everybody."

It's not that we haven't kissed in public before. We've been kissing and making out a lot (to a degree), and sometimes other people are in the vicinity. If I had my way, I'd clear out Central Park for just the two of us, but I know that's not about to happen, so I haven't minded when he's kissed me in places like that. Because I can't wait, either. I'm always wanting to be close to him, in a way that scares me and occasionally makes me feel very, very happy.

But this time was different. He was kissing me to prove a point, and I felt beside the point.

We're walking past the doorman station, and Gabriel's nowhere to be found.

"I should call the super," Ely says. "It's not that I dislike the guy—he's great. But it usually helps to have the doorman somewhere in the vicinity of the door."

I've always wondered why there aren't any female doormen (doorpeople? door attendants?) in New York City. It's the last stronghold of Big Apple sexism, I guess. Nobody seems to mind it. Like it's fine for a woman behind a reception desk to buzz you up or arrange a cab or call the police if you stagger in bleeding, but put her in a doorway and she'd presumably turn into a sobbing, helpless wreck. I want to ask Ely about this, but then I realize I'm sidetracking.

"Really," I say, "why did you kiss me in front of everybody?"

Ely looks at me like I'm more than an idiot but less than a genius, and says, "Could you possibly believe it's because at that moment I just wanted to kiss you, and I didn't care who saw?"

Is that it? He's certainly done it before—that spontaneous grab, that sharp detour into a dark doorway, that naughty (naughty!) ear-bite in the back of a cab. Just last night, he was kissing me at an ATM, delaying my transaction, hitting the button to translate it into Russian and Chinese (or was it Japanese?) so we would keep on speaking in tongues. I was so conscious of the cameras, of the thought that we were on some grainy videotape loop that a security guy monitoring the loop for two dollars an hour in India was going to post on the Web. It was a performance, but it was ultimately okay, because it was an anonymous performance. Not like at bingo, with everyone seeing.

But maybe it's just me. Because I'll admit it: Whenever

he does it, whenever he so clearly wants me, there's this un-
deniable part of me that's thinking, *Why?* I am so much
more Napoleon than dynamite, so much more Play-Doh than
Playguy. He's a twink and I'm a Twinkie, and I can never forget that. Never for one moment can I feel comfortable when
he is so much more beautiful and so much more experienced
than me. I wonder if this is why we've gone nowhere near having sex yet. Maybe the worst thing about me asking about the
kiss is that I can't believe that I alone am a good enough reason.

He doesn't seem bothered by the question, though. Just a
little bewildered. And since he's always a little bewildered, it
blends into the early evening. It's not quite dark yet and we're
headed up to the Museum of Natural History, since it's open
late on Fridays and you can pay what you want without feeling like you're cheating the mummies of their suggested retail
price.

I haven't gotten to talk to Ely all day, and I know I have to.
It wasn't the right time when I showed up at his apartment,
since his moms were having a tense moment and Ely was ex-
cited to show me the model he was making for his architecture
class. Then there was bingo, where I kept spacing, thinking
about what happened this morning—I think I actually had
bingo about four calls before I said I did, but I wasn't paying
enough attention to be sure. I was also hoping Mrs. Loy would
say, "I'm knackered, you ponce!" which is something I've always wanted to work into conversations but never quite manage to. Like *bollocks.* Such a great word, no way to really use
it. Not in my life, at least.

"Are you ready for 'Smell!'?" Ely asks, since that's where we're going—this megapopular exhibit about smell that everybody's been talking about.

"I gave myself a nostril enema just this morning," I tell him.

He laughs. And I love when he laughs, because he's not one of those people who laughs at just anything. You have to earn an Ely laugh, and when I'm with him, I actually find myself saying things that are laughworthy. I enjoy myself more.

And, yes, all of that scares me, too.

I don't see why I don't tell him right now, before we get to the museum. But I feel so silly, so childish, to be so worried. This is something Ely's already gone through, probably before he learned how to walk. I am such an amateur.

If I keep talking, if I keep joking, Ely won't know what I'm thinking, what I'm worried about. He doesn't really know me enough yet to see the warning signs, to take one look and know to say, "Hey, what's wrong?" I've never had that with anyone, really. Just myself. I always know my signs.

Conversation turns, as it often does, to Naomi.

"I just don't get it," he says. "Other Bruce was perfect for her—the perfect hydrant. Hopelessly devoted." He pauses. "But I guess it *does* make sense, in a way. She thrives on conflict. And probably the only conflict she ever got out of him was when she was debating with herself about dumping him."

I hate this. I feel like it's all my fault. He is so hurt. He admitted it at first—that first week when he was waiting for her to call, waiting for the dove to appear over the ocean. At the beginning of the week, he'd jump up for every ringtone . . . even if we were making out, even if we were somewhere awkward, like a movie or a restaurant. Then, as the days passed, he turned wistful. He'd hear the phone and say, "Maybe it's her." He'd finish what he was doing before checking. But he was still disappointed when it wasn't her.

The week mark was clearly a milestone. Once the friendship breakdown finished its Sabbath, once they had their PO box pissing match, things started to get ugly. He gave in and texted her a simple *So, you don't have anything to say to me?* And then—two days later—her response:

I don't.

So he decided he didn't, either. And they wouldn't. So they haven't.

Ely swears up and down that it doesn't have anything to do with me, that their friendship is much too big a thing to have ended over a boy.

I hope that's true.

I don't believe it.

I tried to talk to Naomi myself. She never picked up. I left voice mails saying I was sorry, telling her that it hadn't been working, explaining that it wasn't anything planned, but it was something I had to do. My apologies probably lasted longer than our relationship. In the few times we'd run into each other—like at bingo—she tucked me next to Ely under her emotional invisibility cloak. As if I was a part of him now, lost in the land of the banished.

The "Smell!" exhibit isn't as crowded as we thought it

would be. There's a huge horizontal nose at the beginning that can be entered through the nostrils. Even though some of the people around us look very serious, like they're smell professors or something, we can't help but act like we're eight-year-old booger fetishists.

"If your nose is runny!" Ely shouts.

"You may think it's funny!" I shout.

"But it's snot!" we shout together.

We play with some supersized cilia, then passage through some nasal cavities. When we get out, Ely pulls me aside and looks all earnest.

"I have a question," he says, touching me lightly on the arm. The gesture is the opposite of the hasty bingo kiss. Under the light of a glowing mucous membrane, I brace myself for whatever's coming next.

"You don't have to answer if you don't want to," he continues, moving closer, looking me right in the eye. "But I just wonder . . . would you still love me if my name was Gland?"

I can't stop or save myself. I say, "I'd love you even if your first name was Gland and your last name was Ular. I'd love you even if your name was Excretion."

"Serious?" he asks.

"Serious," I say.

This is how I can do it—how we can do it—being serious in an unserious way.

But still . . . there is the real serious underneath.

The next room is full of perfumes and an explanation of

how perfumes are made. I'm a little disturbed by the origin of ambergris, but I get over it. Then we hit the nose amplifiers, where you can plug in your nostrils and breathe in different scents. Everything else is blocked out, like using headphones in your ears. I try some out (the plugs are one-use-only, much to my hygienic relief) and am dosed up with the deepest, purest almond I've ever experienced, including taste. Then I stupidly stop and smell the coffee, and I can't block out the morning anymore. It's there, and I can't escape what it means.

I must be standing at the station for too long. I feel Ely's hand on my shoulder, hear him say, "Hey, be careful—too much of that and you won't sleep tonight."

I take the plugs out and throw them away. But even if the scent dissipates, the thoughts don't. In some way, Ely and I cross over, because he sees this, and even if he doesn't say, "Hey, what's wrong?" he clearly recognizes that there's something wrong, and he isn't going to sidetrack me or sidetrack himself until he knows I'm okay.

So I tell him, "I think I came out to my mother this morning."

Why did I think he would laugh? Why did I think he would say, "Oh, that's not so bad?" Why did I think it was important only to me?

"Oh, Bruce," he says, and then he just reaches up and moves his thumb gently under my eye, wiping the tear that feels like it's been hanging there all day.

There are too many people around me, and I say that, and Ely takes me to a quieter room, one of the diorama rooms that nobody really visits anymore, detailing the everyday life of a 1950s Eskimo. We sit on a bench, and he holds my hand and asks me what happened.

And maybe it isn't as bad as I've felt, because I actually smile even though I'm crying a little again, and I say, "It's actually because of your name."

I tell him about how it was just a regular morning, with my dad already at work and my mom having her morning coffee. I slept over to do some laundry and get some work done away from the dorm. We usually talk about classes and things, but this morning, her first question was:

"Who's Ellie?"

And I didn't get it at first. I said, "Ellie?"

It was only when she followed up with "What happened to that Naomi girl?" that I knew who she meant.

"It didn't work out with Naomi," I told her, thinking that would be the end of it.

But no. She continued with "Well, that must make Ellie something else."

I must have looked like a deer caught in a head vise, because Mom put her mug down and said, "I'm sorry. I needed the number for that doctor I called on your phone last week when mine was dead. So I looked on your call log, and I couldn't help but notice there were a lot of calls to Ellie. I know, I know—I should have asked you. But you were asleep, and I thought you'd be more annoyed with me for waking you up. I really needed the number. My back is killing me again."

The bizarre thing was, knowing my mother's mind after

experiencing eighteen years of its effects, I was sure this story was completely true. The line-crossing came when she thought she could bring it up with me.

Still, I could've let it go. I could have just said, "It's a friend." Or "It's no one."

But I didn't want to lie. I didn't want to tell the truth, but I really didn't want to lie.

So I said, "It's *Ely*, Mom. A guy."

And then

I added

"He's my kind-of boyfriend."

I feel a little sheepish telling this to Ely now, since we haven't even had the b-word conversation. But he doesn't dispute it. Instead he asks, "What did she say?"

And I tell him she said, "Does this mean that you're gay?" Too shocked to sound disapproving or accepting.

And I answered, "No. It just means I'm not straight."

It was so obvious that neither of us was at all prepared to have this conversation, and neither of us had expected to have it at that particular moment, over that particular mug of coffee.

Then, the weirdest thing of all, the morning continued. I'd clearly altered something, but the shape of that alteration couldn't be known yet. She didn't say, "I love you," and she didn't say, "I hate you." She just said, "I'm sorry I looked at your phone," and I said, "It's okay. Did you get the appointment?" And she asked, "What?" and I said, "For the doctor," and she nodded and said, "One o'clock, during lunch," and I said, "That was lucky."

We had no idea what we were doing.

"So," I say to Ely now, "I don't know what I'm going to go home to, the next time I go home. I don't even know if my mom's going to tell my dad."

"Do you want me to go over there with you?"

I shake my head and tell him no, it's probably not the best time for him to meet my parents.

He laughs. I feel a centimeter better.

"I guess you didn't really have to go through this," I say to him.

"I did, actually," he tells me, his feet kicking playfully into mine. "It was definitely different, but it still *completely* freaked me out."

At the risk of stating the obvious, I ask, "But why? You have two moms."

"But that's exactly why," Ely says. "It's so hard to explain. It was just so *expected* in a way. They tried so hard when I was growing up to make sure my world wasn't entirely a queer one—not that they were ashamed of who they were or anything. Not at all. But they wanted me to have the same kind of options as any other kid. And I think part of me agreed— I wanted to be different from them. I would be the normal—no, *normal* isn't the right word. I would be the more conventional one, I guess. I convinced myself of all these things I wanted— to play for the Yankees, to have this big wedding with Naomi, to bring home this girl to my moms so they'd finally have a daughter. I really thought it would happen, that I could do it. I didn't want all the other kids thinking I was only being gay because my moms were gay. I tried to be straight. Isn't that stupid? Me? But I did. It was a fun fantasy. But at the end of the day, it was the boys I wanted to kiss. You still have your options, but I knew that something—I don't know what—had already defined me. I just had to figure out the definition and be okay with it.

"When I finally realized I had to be who I was going to be, Mom and Mom were also a little freaked out. They were worried I was doing it as some way of proving I was on their side. I actually had to persuade them that I was really, truly, genuinely into penis. *That* was a fun conversation!"

"I'm not sure I'll bring that up tonight with my parents," I say, noting to myself that my experiences with penis have still been limited to my own.

"Yeah—save the buggery conversation for a better occasion, like Thanksgiving."

"Bollocks!" I say. It feels good.

"Bollocks?"

"Yeah, bollocks."

"Now would be a good time to admit you're on crack."

"I'm sorry. Continue."

It's Ely's turn to look sheepish. "There isn't much more to it," he admits. "Once my true rainbow colors came shining through, the moms did everything short of writing me a profile on xy.com. I mean, there was this one time when I was looking at this naked picture of a guy on my computer, and then I got a phone call or something and forgot to close it, and Mom Susan went to use the computer before I could close the window. I figured she was going to be all mad, but instead all she said was 'Ely, you *know* how little that does for me.' "

I try to imagine my mother having a similar reaction, but I can't.

"Don't worry," Ely says. "I've dated other guys who've gone through this. It always ends up fine. I mean, this one guy, Ono, was kicked out of his house. But you're not living at home, and I'm sure your parents are much cooler than Ono's. His dad threatened to call the police. Seriously. He said, 'Dad, I'm gay,' and his father shouted that he was going to call the police."

I can't say I completely appreciate this sidetrack, but he's trying in his own Ely way, just as I'm trying to keep the "other guys" out of our Eskimo room.

"Should we head out?" I ask.

"Sure," Ely says, standing up and offering me his hand. When I take it, he yanks me up and doesn't let go. I'm almost afraid he's going to want to kiss me or make out or even hug me right now. It would feel wrong, and I think he realizes this. So he just spins me around once, like we're dancing. Then, when I trip, he says, "Eskimo two-step," and instead of laughing looks at me again to see if I'm okay.

I let go of his hand, and we start walking back. We detour by the dinosaurs and the blue whale and the birds of paradise. We talk about other things, especially the people around us.

It's only when we're heading out the door and down the front steps of the museum that Ely says to me, seemingly out of the blue, "You know, I'm proud to be your kind-of boyfriend."

"Bollocks!" I scream out into the night.

"Not bollocks!" Ely calls back.

And for that moment, my heart is lifting too fast to be scared of falling.

STARBUCKS

NAOMI

Starbucks: It's where life happens.

Someone should totally hire me to write slogans.

People come to New York to be different, but I go to Starbucks to be the same.

Go to a Starbucks in Kansas City or one in Manhattan, and I am confident that pretty much the same experience will be had in either. Same decor. Same dependably boring coffee. Same underpaid workers grateful to have health insurance. Same crap World Music playing that's supposed to make you believe the ©orporation believes in fair-trade values.

Starbucks: the great equalizer.

No, I liked the first slogan better.

Ely is better than me at everything except Starbucks. That's why we could only meet here.

He arrives late and slumps down into the chair I've reserved for him at the ♿ end of the table. It was the only empty seat left in the whole place, and if a person in a wheelchair rolls in, then everyone else here might resent Ely as much as I do right now.

"I didn't realize you meant *this* Starbucks," Ely says. He ignores the Frappuccino I've left on the table for him. Ely hates Frappuccinos. Something about a bad-boy hangover and bad spew chunks after the bad boy very badly dumped him. "I thought Astor Place was off-limits to my cooties? I've been waiting for you at the one across St. Marks for the last twenty minutes. Did you not see my text messages? Or are you so passive-aggressive now that you won't even answer my text messages?"

No, I'm so passive-aggressive that I didn't even bother turning on my phone.

⌛

"You're kidding me with this, right, Naomi?"

⌛

"You're not even going to *speak* to me?"

We can do this without speaking.

I'm not here for angry recrimination: *You stole my boyfriend, Ely! Stole my trust—in YOU, not in him.*

I can't speak, because I've run out of lies.

If I say now what I really feel, Naomi & Ely really never will be Naomi & Ely again.

Why did it take you stealing my boyfriend to make me finally understand that you will never love me the way I love you?

If I did speak, I'd probably say something scary and stupid, like "I always imagined our daughter having your beautiful eyes and possibly my chin and hopefully not Ginny's nose. Susan's laugh and my mom's great hair. She'd have your math skills and my distrust of prime-numbered streets. Her soul would be her own. We'd protect it always, together."

When does the hurt stop? I need a timetable.

Ely's not waiting on ⧗. He sets down the first item—my "girl kit" of feminine supplies I kept in what was my drawer in his room, but now the drawer has probably been claimed by Bruce the Second's stuff. "I can't wait forever, Naomi. Let's get this over with. Even if you've gone mute, I'm sure your hands still have the capability to cough up your end of the bargain."

Ely's face looks too flush. I think he's coming down with a cold. I should have chosen the Starbucks on St. Marks. They keep the temperature four degrees higher. Why am I such a bitch?

I still can't speak, but I do reach down to the box of his stuff that I've placed on the floor.

If you could offer me a guarantee, Ely, a guarantee that the hurt that makes my heart feel like a boulder sitting inside my chest, beatless, if I knew this hurt would eventually go away and I could feel hope again—for me, for you, for us—then maybe my lips could ⧓ now and we could get on with this. The End.

ELY

I remember this feeling. When Mom Susan discovered that Mom Ginny was having an affair with Naomi's dad . . . I remember thinking, *Is this it? Is it all over?* I thought, *Are they going to split up?* My parents. Naomi's parents. And I realized— no, *realized* is the wrong word. *Realized* makes it sound like a fact I learned rather than a fact I felt. So let me say *knew*. I *knew* for the first time that when you say a couple is splitting up, it's not just the relationship that's splitting. In some way, everyone involved gets split up, too. Each of my moms was splitting. Each of Naomi's parents was splitting. Naomi was splitting. I was splitting. And the reaction to that—my reaction to that—was to hold on as strong as possible. To try to hold things together. Because to let go would be the end of everything. To let go would be a murder of what once was.

Maybe Naomi and I haven't learned anything. Or maybe your history just repeats and repeats until it batters you enough to snap the seams that hold you together. I don't know. All I know is that this feels wrong. But if she won't talk to me, there's no way to make it right.

I am so mad at her.

What we're doing is, technically, the opposite of splitting. We're reuniting our possessions. Returning them to the rightful owners. As if some kind of iron curtain fell in the hallway between our apartments and we're exchanging the refugees.

"Here," I say, handing over her I ♥ JAKE RYAN T-shirt and her Pokémon watch and her *Dawson's Creek* DVDs and her

Hello Kitty pajamas—the ones where I wrote in a mouth on every damn Hello Kitty because it always freaked both of us out that Hello Kitty had no way to speak, like a cartoon geisha vulnerable to any dog who came along.

She takes everything I put on the table and doesn't say a word.

"How are things with Gabriel?" I ask. Rumor has it he's gotten a bad case of the Naomis, to the point that he was overheard whistling "Signed, Sealed, Delivered" when she checked her mail the other day.

No answer.

"Things with Bruce are great," I say. "Thanks for asking."

Truth: Things with Bruce feel precarious, although I don't know why. I find myself wondering what he's thinking much more often than I ever have with any boy.

I know it's not exactly good form to mention Bruce to Naomi, but all I'm looking for is a reaction here. Any reaction.

But instead she dumps a bag of my own possessions onto the table.

When he laughs, I want to laugh, too. I almost smile back.

He's looking at our favorite panel of Hello Kitty cartoon bubbles, on the left shoulder side of the pajama top. In Ely's handwriting, one Kitty purrs, "Me love you long time." The next Kitty, in my handwriting, points out, "No nice kitty appreciate racist stereotype." The last Kitty, rounding the shoulder in Ely's scribble, promises, "I would be most delighted to give you pleasure at the time of your convenience."

Now seems the appropriate time for the movie exchange. I take out our shared classic and return it to him.

"I really didn't need this back," Ely says, reaching for the DVD of *Mount Fuckmore*. "Watching straight people have sex really creeps me out."

We found the DVD in a trash can on the street the summer after ninth grade; the find merited a sleepover at his apartment that night while the parents were out. And if I want to laugh now, it's not at the sight of Ely sitting in the world's most wholesome beverage establishment, holding up what I swear to Lincoln and Jefferson combined is the *filthiest* DVD cover in the history of our forefathers. I want to laugh because I'm remembering that first time we watched *Mount Fuckmore*, when Ely hit pause at the grossest part and turned to me to ask, "You know that song about *You're a grand old flag, you're a high-flying flag*?" and I was like, "Yeah?" and he said, "Well, that part where it goes *Every heart beats true 'neath the red, white, and blue / Where there's never a boast or brag*?" and I was like, "Yeah?" and he goes, "Well, that's totally false. The *whole song* is about boasting and bragging!" and I was like, "Yeah, you're a genius!" and we fell out of his bed, we laughed so hard.

I refuse to take the DVD back. Much as I can't help but be intrigued by porn, at the same time, watching it makes me feel unbearably sad and empty inside. Like there's nothing left to wish for.

Discovering *Mount Fuckmore* at too tender an age is probably what screwed me so badly with men. I mean, yeah, there's the whole parent situation, and the Ely baggage, and the weird convergence of my looks and my body and my bitch streak, plus the ick way ick men have been looking at me since I was fourteen. But I blame *Mount Fuckmore*.

I could give less of a fuck how Bruce and Ely are. But how does Ely know about Gabriel?

How much of a loser am I, anyway? The hottest doorman in the history of our forefathers and their foreskins really likes me, like *like-likes* me, and I can't like him back, because I'm overwhelmed with grief, and also, I know if I like him back, if I let it happen, I will fuck it up. And then I won't just have to avoid my former best friend across the hall, I'll also have to avoid the entrance and exit of my building. Which would be awkward as well as logistically impossible.

But, Mr. Lincoln? Hello? Gabriel is sooooo cute. Honestly. I sooooo want to let it happen.

I sooooo wish I had clue one as to what I am supposed to make of the mix Gabriel gave me.

"Is that my glitter belt?" Ely asks.

I don't want Ely to take back the belt. I want him to say I should keep it. It's the belt that binds us. If I keep it—if he offers—then maybe not all hope is lost.

I nod.

Ely reaches for the belt.

ELY

I have to know it's pretty bad when the sight of glitter depresses me. I guess I just wanted to see it one more time. Then I move it over to her box.

"You can have it," I say.

It's sad that I don't want it anymore.

The things I want, I've kept. All of the notes and letters we've passed to each other. The place-mat drawings she'd give to me like a proud kindergartner every time we went to a restaurant where there were crayons. The pipe-cleaner jewelry we made for each other. The NYU sweatshirt she bought me when she found out I'd gotten in; her mail came a day later, and I had to hop on the subway to reciprocate immediately. I can give her back her tampons and her porn and her hair clips and her Plath and her Sexton. But some things have to remain mine, or else the falling apart will be too complete.

I can't do this anymore. I push the box back in her direction.

"Just keep it all," I say. "Or throw it out. Or give it to Housing Works. Or mail it to some orphanage for fellow mutes. If you wanted to make me even more miserable, you've succeeded beautifully. I hope you're really proud of yourself. Bravo."

I get up to leave.

This is so much worse than I imagined.

He's actually crying as he stands up to leave. He's not outright sobbing like the pathetic fool I feel like right now, but tears spot his flushed cheeks and his eyes are wet and he is insistent on staring straight into my gaze—he will not back down or look away. It's like he's squeezing every last ounce of matter from my heart.

In the future, I vow to never, ever again take advice from Bruce the First. The stuff exchange was his latest insomniac idea, and I went along with it when he proposed it to Ely, mostly to ease my conscience over toying with the high school boy's affections. Also, the curiosity.

Also, I miss Ely so bad.

I push the plastic bag of Ely and I have lifted from various restaurants over the years in his direction. I kept the collection of coffee creamers we've stolen from restaurants for myself. Ely doesn't seem to notice the discrepancy.

I miss Dad, too.

I've gotten used to it.

I just don't see the way out for Naomi & Ely. Or the way back in.

"You really have nothing at all left to say, Naomi?" His eyes plead, *Please don't do this, Naomi. There's still time to back down.* "I can't believe you'd give up everything we have together over a guy."

I have to do this. How can Ely not understand that? Why

does he think this is all about him and Bruce? The guy was just the catalyst. It's my entire belief system of planning the Naomi & Ely future together that's in shreds now.

There's plenty of room for me on the empty side of Mom's bed of despair. I hope it doesn't take me as long as her to snap out of it and move on.

How come Ely never wanted me? At least once? What's wrong with me?

Finally I have words to speak. I place my hand on the red glitter belt. *My* red glitter belt. *Thank you, Ely.* "The belt really does look better on me," I say.

And here is why I will love Ely to my dying breath. He laughs.

Snot runs down his nose. I hand him a Kleenex. Somehow I think he's never looked more beautiful. Teary-eyed, splotchy-cheeked, runny-nosed, laughing and crying. My boy.

ELY

"Are you going to talk to me now?" I ask. Who ever thought that getting her to speak a single line of sarcastic banter would be such a challenge?

She just shakes her head, gives me that sad smile.

Fine. I figure I'll take what I can get. And maybe just a little bit more.

That's the way it is with me.

Naomi understands. Or at least I have to think she does.

We never really did play well with others. Only each other. Maybe that's another reason this is so hard. Or so stupid. Or so necessary. Or all three.

"I gotta go," I say. Then I leave a space for her to say "Don't." I leave a space for her to say "This is hard" or "This is stupid" or "This is necessary." I leave a space for her to get up and kiss me on the cheek. Or tell me to open the bag of crayons so we can graffiti over the abandoned latte cups. Or tell me there's been some mistake.

But instead she says nothing. Not even "good-bye."

And because she gives me nothing, I give her nothing back.

Hard, stupid, and necessary.

LIKEWISE

Today is the first day of the rest of my life. Today is the first day of the rest of my life.

Now if the juggler entertaining the tourist crowd in the middle of Washington Square Park would just stay *still* for a moment, I'd have a better view through my binoculars as to the identity of the persons sharing a bench with Naomi at the other end of the park. I already know the *where* of Naomi in her life after Me; if I could just know the *who*, I'd have the closure I need to move on with the rest of my life.

Tomorrow may have to settle for ringing in the first day of the rest of my life.

The chess players nearby are antsy—they want my table. But Cutie Pie is having a nice nap on top of the game table where I'm sitting. She's basking in the sun shining onto her contented face. I wouldn't dare move her. Who am I to disturb peaceful sleep? I can only envy it. I can only envy Mrs. Loy's sleep, as well. She's sitting on a bench a few yards away from our table, holding her cane, her chin lodged on her chest.

"You're not a very good stalker."

The voice comes from behind me. I turn around. Oh no.

I set the binoculars in my lap, on top of Mrs. Loy's hand-bag, placed there for safekeeping during her nap. He hesitates for a moment—at least!—like he knows the better instinct would be to act as if we'd never noticed one another. If he had any decency whatsoever, he'd acknowledge we'd prefer not to acknowledge each other for one more agonizing second by just walking away.

But oh yes. He sits down on the empty bench opposite me. Why does the universe hate me?

"What are you doing here?" I ask Bruce the Second. I line up the chess figures in opening rank-and-file positions. He could make himself useful, at least.

"I just had a class in that building over there." He points in the direction of a school building on the Naomi side of the park. He places his hand on a pawn. "I can't make an opening move unless you move him." He points at the sleeping Chihuahua.

"Cutie Pie's a girl."

No respect for good sleep. He reaches over to the dog and lifts her into the air, his hand underneath her stomach. "Nothing to brag about here," he says, "but if you examine more carefully, you'll see she is in fact a he."

I verify. Bruce the Second wasn't kidding about Cutie Pie having nothing to brag about.

The dog has no loyalty, either. Cutie Pie nestles himself into Bruce the Second's lap to resume his nap.

I move my rook. Since we're already on the subject of

fluctuating sexuality, I inform Bruce the Second, "You don't look gay." Chinos and a Lacoste shirt? Come *on*.

"How is gay supposed to look?"

"Not like you."

"Thanks for the vote of confidence."

"What music do you like?"

"Why do I have the feeling this is a gay quiz?"

"Because maybe it is."

"Then I don't know. I like lots of different types of music, but I'm not obsessive about it like Ely is. I like classical. I like the Beatles." I guess this Bruce isn't entirely awful, because he notices my disappointed expression and adds, "And I guess I like a few Madonna songs?"

"At least." *Please.* Classical? The Beatles? Someone needs to reprogram this guy's musical preferences to the rainbow channel.

"At least *you*, Bruce, could elevate yourself above looking like a stalker, if you tried," he says as he captures my bishop. I'm really off my game.

"I'm trying, dude. I'm trying."

I feel like he believes me. He should. I meant what I said, even if I can't seem to accomplish trying's goal—getting over Naomi. He asks, "If I tell you who she's over there talking with, will that help?"

"No." Pause. "Yes."

"She's sitting there with Robin from Schenectady and another guy—"

"Gabriel?"

"No, not Gabriel. Why would you think Gabriel?"

Ha-ha, is it possible I have information that has not yet infiltrated to Ely?

I say, "Gabriel likes Naomi. He gave her a mix he made her and they are always gazing at each other at the mailboxes, but then she hardly has like two words to say to him. Supposedly she made a mix for him in return, but it was all like Z100-type shit and he was horrified—"

"Horrified to realize she must have gotten all her musical cool and knowledge from Ely?"

"Exactly."

"Actually, I think Ely knows about this Gabriel thing." Damn. "But since Naomi refuses to speak to him"—Naomi and Ely's freeze is totally okay with me, by the way—"I doubt Ely is planning to help Naomi through this one."

I'm fairly sure I loathe and despise this guy, but the universe must acknowledge the universal truth: It's easy talking with another Bruce. Almost comforting.

"How do you know all this about Naomi and Gabriel?" he asks me.

"Naomi's mom told me." Naomi's not speaking to *me* anymore, either, but she hasn't frozen me out like she has Ely. I'm allowed to e-mail and text-message with her, but I am not to speak with or acknowledge her when we're in the building. Not communicating with me verbally is part of her Tough Love campaign, she informed me. To help me move on, like she has to from Ely. According to my sister, Kelly, Naomi's doing us all a public service. Maybe she is. I don't know. Maybe I need to sleep on it.

"I find that hard to believe," Bruce says.

"Naomi's mom counts on me for Ambien. Believe it."

"That's illegal."

"So are the five hundred drug deals being transacted in this park while we play chess."

"Do you think the tourists having their wallets pick-pocketed while they watch the juggler will notice sooner, or later?"

"Later."

"I agree," Bruce the Second agrees. Then: "I'm worried," he says.

"About me?"

"No, *you'll* be fine. You need to dump the binoculars and make a friend within your own age range, maybe realize you're a nice and good-looking kid whom probably several girls you already know at school would really like to get to know better if you'd stop comparing them to Naomi . . . but otherwise, you're all right."

"Thanks." I think. Since he seems to want to know me better, I add, "As one great man wrote, 'I am nothing special; of this I am sure. I am just a common man with common thoughts. There are no monuments dedicated to me and my name will soon be forgotten. But I've loved another with all my heart and soul, and to me, that has always been enough.' "

"Aristotle?"

"Nicholas Sparks."

"Which one?"

"*The Notebook.*"

"I cried at the end of *A Walk to Remember.*"

"Book or movie?"

"Movie."

"The book was better."

We're given our own walk to remember as a white-boy Rastafarian approaches our table. "Yeah?" the Rasta goes. His hands make a movement for his front pants pocket, but we both know this is not a pervert walkabout.

"NO!" both Bruces go.

Whitey-boy Rasta moves on to the next table, and Bruce the Second says, "*That's* what I'm worried about. The guy sitting on the bench with Robin and Naomi on the other side of the park happens to be the resident dealer to most of the NYU dorms."

"How do you know?"

"My freshman roommate got kicked out of the dorm for possession of marijuana he bought from that guy sitting over there with Robin and Naomi."

"No way!" I consider the situation, then impart my conclusion: "Nah, I wouldn't worry. I could see Naomi possibly being into more drug experimentation, but that Robin girl from Schenectady, she's way too boring and straightlaced to let Naomi do that."

"Unless Robin is desperate to break out of her straightlaced version of herself?"

"Kind of like you have?"

I don't mean the comment as an insult, and he doesn't take it as one. He laughs. "Kind of," he allows. "Only I'd like to think I held the desperate part in check." His next chess move allows him to add, "Check."

I don't know why, but I'm relieved I didn't offend him. Still, we're all suffering because of The Situation. I need to know if it's worth it. "Do you love him?" I ask Bruce the Second.

His hands cover his queen while deciding where to move her, and how to answer. "I might," he says.

I have to know. "What's that like?"

I mean the love part, not the sex part—I *really* don't want to hear about that. And instinctually he seems to understand this. He answers with a happy glow, not a horny glow, looking right at me, as only one Bruce can do to another. "It's amazing." He looks down, blushing a little, and pats the dog. When his eyes move back up to meet mine, he adds, "It's also scary. *Really* scary."

And instinctually I know he means the love part over the gay part. Rock covers paper.

The kind of glow on Bruce's face is one I've never felt for Naomi. With Naomi, it was not amazing. Or scary. I guess it wasn't love. It was a *mission*. Scissors cut paper.

One more thing. Bruce the Second says, "It's amazing, and scary, and Ely and I would be enjoying it much more if it weren't for Naomi."

"Eh." I shrug. "She'll get over it." Like I will. I think I can believe.

"I hope so. But it doesn't feel good to see her hurting so badly. Ely and I did everything we possibly could to right the wrong with her, but she wouldn't have it. There's nothing more I can do here. I think I'm going to just work on getting Ely's moms to like me, for the time being. They might be an easier hurdle to cross than Naomi."

Mount Everest might be an easier hurdle to cross than Naomi.

One more thing I have to know. "Have the moms invited you to Sunday brunch?"

"Yes."

"Then you're in."

He smiles and hands Cutie Pie over to me. Then he makes his move. "Checkmate. And I have econ class in fifteen minutes on this side of the park." He stands up.

"You're a decent Bruce, Bruce," I tell Bruce.

He smiles again. I should buy him a designer shirt from one of Mom's salesclerk friends at Bendel for his birthday or something, to help gay up his wardrobe.

"Thanks, Bruce," he says. "Likewise."

FRIENDS

So I was talking to my man Gerald and I was saying, Look, there's this girl, and the stupid thing is I can really talk to her and all that shit without getting freaked out or spaced, and he was like, That's all good, and I was telling him that, yeah, I could really trust her and I knew she was really into me and really into the same films and whatever, and Gerald was like, What's the problem? and I was saying, The thing is, if I had my way, she'd always keep her clothes on, which made him say, So she's a dog, and I was like, No, no, no, you don't get it, she's completely cute in a cute way and if I didn't know her, I might do her, but I do know her and because I know her I don't want to do her, I just want to do shit like talk to her and drink with her and sit and do homework with her, because when we do shit like that, it's not nearly as boring as it is when I do it alone, because every now and then she'll grunt or laugh and I'll say, What? and she'll come up with the most random shit, which totally makes me think she's the greatest, only I don't want to sleep with her. And Gerald, he was saying, Dude, you know there's a word for that kind of relationship, and I was like,

Please tell me what it is because this is *killing me,* and Gerald was smiling and taking a big drag before he said to me, Friendship, man—that shit's called friendship. And that really set me straight, or at least I thought it did, because it was so fucking obvious and I figured it would be obvious to her and we'd be okay with it, but then I kept getting these fucked-up moments from her where it felt like she was trying to make it something other than friendship—like always putting her hand on my shoulder or asking me for a back rub and once saying, It's a date! when I asked her to go see this Fassbinder thing at Anthology. And I thought, *Dude, you're probably overreacting, because this girl is smart, and no way is she wanting to get with a fuckup like you.* But it kept being out there, and the thing was, even though I really liked her as a person, I didn't really think I liked her as a girl, because when you like a girl, there's this ignition—you can feel it—and with her, there wasn't any ignition, just conversation and hanging out and shit. So one night after we saw *La Dolce Vita* at Film Forum, we went out for drinks, and I think she waited until I was three drinks in, because my head was like a Jell-O shot when she asked something like What's going on with us? and I was like, We're the Robin Super Twins, or something dumb like that, and she was like, No, that's not a good answer. Let me repeat myself, what am I to you? and even if I had been one hundred percent sober, I don't know if I could've answered, because I hate it when you have to give definitions to things that are bigger than definitions—which is a compliment to her, but she didn't really take it that way. I got what she was really asking, and I thought about when Gerald and I were talking, and how simple it seemed then. I'm not brain-dead—I knew that introducing that particular f-word into the conversation would be poison, because when a girl asks you if you wanna go out, the last thing they want is for you to say how great your friendship is, which sucks, because you can *totally* mean it in the *best possible way,* but it still sounds like you're handing her a sack of shit. I couldn't think of anything else to say, because I wasn't about to say Hey, Robin, there's nothing about you that makes me pop a boner, so I said, You're my friend, and I meant it, and she took it just as badly as I knew she would, only instead of crying or trying to call me on it, she just took her drink and launched it into my face. Man, I've had plenty of beer spilled on me, but this was completely different—not only was I sticky afterward, but I went into this meta-shock, because while the physical act of what just happened was bad, it was the more existential *Someone just threw a drink in my face* that really got top billing. I half thought she was going to throw the glass at me, too. Or say fuck you. But instead she just said, Enough, and looked at me for a second with this laser-beam glare, and at that moment—pow!—*total* ignition. She was sexy as hell, and she was sexy as hell because she had no idea that she was doing it. Her hand was shaking when she put the glass back down on the table and she was clearly as surprised as me by the drink throwing, but the cool thing was she was going to go through with it, she was just going to ride her anger right the hell out of the bar, and I knew there was no chance I could get her to stay, and I was sad because not only was I losing the one decent friend in my life, I was also losing this friend I suddenly wanted to make out with. She left me with the check, which was completely unfair, because she knows all my drug money goes straight to my film fund (fuck digital), but it was worth every maxed-out credit card to see her storm like that. I knew what I had to do—text her, call her, e-mail her, and give her every possible chance to turn me down. If I could get her back easy, it wouldn't be worth it, because it would be the same as before. But if she put up a fight—if she really got to feeling fire for me—well, then, that was something else. I bombarded her at first, and hit the wall of silence pretty fast. A good sign. Then I unleashed the second wave—all the I'm-so-stupid shit. Got her to tell me to stop. Then I stopped. Put up my own wall of silence, but made it clear that I'd left a ladder for her. I just needed some-one to point it out, and that's where Naomi—hot, sexy, heartbreaking, mindfuck-central Naomi—came in. We'd been talking about doing a movie together for a while, just me fol-lowing her around, seeing the city from her p.o.v. Like reality TV, only real. She has star quality—bright and pointed. And, best for me, I knew she and Robin were talking a lot, espe-cially since Naomi just lost her gay best friend. So I called her up and said, Yeah, we should get together and see if we're really going to do this thing, and it was perfect, because Naomi was all like, You're just trying to do this to get Robin back, and at first I was like, No, no, no—I waited a good ten minutes until I was telling her, Naomi? You know that thing? You said be-fore? About Robin? What if it's a little true? And she just cracked, offering to help me, telling me I had a chance, wanting to be the one to make it all better. Total friend points. She said, I'm going to be in the park with Robin, so why don't you bump into us at this time and say you want to talk about the movie, and then I'll have to leave for some reason. She even told me to wear my blue shirt, because that was Robin's favorite, and at first I wanted to be like, Bitch, I have about twenty blue shirts, but the cool thing was I knew exactly which one she was talking about, because I'd always thought of it as the one that Robin really liked. Just to be on the safe side, I asked Naomi if Robin was seeing someone else, and for a second she sounded like she had a piece of gum in her throat. Then she told me that it probably wasn't an issue, but I should be on my best behavior anyway. Which is how I ended up getting Gerald to man the ganja hotline so I could just happen to bump into Naomi and Robin in the park this afternoon. When I get to their bench, Naomi goes into this whole monologue about how she's been meaning to call me back about the movie, and I'm careful to be looking at her but also stealing glances at Robin so Robin can see me doing it without thinking I know how obvious I'm being. I'm afraid she's going to leave, but instead she's sending out the vibe that I should be the one who leaves. (Of course, Naomi keeps talking, so I'm in the clear.) She doesn't look happy to see me, which is bad, but she also looks sad to see me, which is good. She always puts up this simple I'm-just-a-girl-from-Schenectady front, but because my dad's from Albany, I happen to know that Schenectady is a town that was built on steel, and if she's the same way, then I'm in for the kind of big trouble that I love. Naomi pauses for a second like she's suddenly realizing how awkward this is, and I know it's my moment to look at Robin directly and say a simple hi. Like a little boy who's like, I know it was wrong to draw on the dining room table with my crayons, and I feel bad about it, and I feel bad and sad that you're angry with me, so now that I've spent an hour in my room, can I please come out now and find that everything's okay again? The thing is, I'm not playing at this—it's really how I feel, because actually seeing her as opposed to thinking about her is incredibly intense and tense, and she's shooting me daggers, but she's not feeling it enough for them to actually hit me, so instead they just fall on the ground in between us, and she's still kind of mad about it, but I'm just like, *Look, daggers!* It is *so* hot, the way she smolders. Naomi's suddenly staring at something, and Robin's all, What? and Naomi says, I see Bruces, which, if I was stoned, would be the most brilliant thing ever, but since I'm on my best behavior, I just think it's odd. I gotta go, Naomi says, and Robin's getting up to go, too, and I say, Please stay for a second, and it's like, holy shit, for the first time in my life, saying please actually gets me something. Naomi heads off and Robin's all, What? again, and I almost want to say, I am so yours it's not even funny. I know you want me, but I want you more. I will stay on my best behavior, because maybe there's a reason it's the best. Maybe there's a reason it had to take this long, because if I'd wanted to sleep with you the first time I met you, it would've never ended up like this. I would have always been the captain.

But now you're in charge. I'm making moves all the time, but only to get you to make that one move. What'll it be? And what I really say is, Naomi sees Bruces everywhere. It's the last thing she expects, and she is amused no matter how much I've disappointed her by wanting to be her friend. I don't like you anymore, she tells me. And I say, I wish you did. She asks why, and this time I have an answer. I tell her, Whether or not you like me, I still like you back. I really like you back. She says, You're an asshole. And I say, Yeah, but I'll be *your* asshole, if you'll have me. (I do *not* say I'll also be her friend. But there's that, too. Yes, there's that.) She snorts, and I think, *That's right, you've got steel.* Then I look at her as straight as I can, and I say, totally cool and totally vulnerable, Hey, let me buy you another drink.

TIGER

Track 1
Bon Jovi: "Livin' on a Prayer"

I don't know what to say to her.

She has such bad taste in music.

So I say, "It's against the co-op board's rules to take naps on the couch in the lobby lounge."

From her fetal position, lying on the lime-green couch, Naomi flashes me that feral look I would never dream of trying to tame. She's more than a little baked, so the hotness of her stare is cooled by the dull glaze around her hazel eyes. "You're not going to give me shit about that, are you?" she asks me.

"Do you need help getting upstairs?" Surely she'd rather sleep in her own bed.

"Please let me sleep it off here instead of up there with Mom."

At four-thirty in the morning, the insomniacs have finally

been put to bed. It'll be another hour before the Wall Street slaves dart through the lobby, shove their dry cleaning at me for pickup by the laundry service later in the morning, then rush out the door to make or lose their millions—or someone else's.

If Naomi stays on that couch, preferably awake, I've got a good hour alone with her. I never know with Naomi whether she wants me to engage her in actual conversation or wants to limit us strictly to text messages and knowing-but-not-knowing glances. There's so much about her I'd genuinely like to know.

"I don't mind if you rest on the couch," I tell Naomi. "But I am bound by the doorman code of conduct to inform you of the co-op board's will."

I can't believe it's my life that I work by a doorman code of conduct. *The co-op board's will.* I can't believe I spoke those words aloud.

Naomi never said a word to me other than "thanks" about the mix I made for her. The one I basically bled my guts onto.

I do recognize that not everyone feels as bound by the implicit playlist-exchange code of conduct as I do. That's why the code is probably implicit only to me.

She must not understand. Greater even than my desire for her to consider me as more than her doorman is my desire—no, my *need*—to hear, in great detail, her every single thought about each single song, each artist, each lyric: Which songs did she like, and why? Which ones has she listened to most and which ones does she find herself skipping over automatically?

The order of the songs—did she notice the flow? Admire the transitions? Feel my beating heart inserted into each track?

Or am I just asking too much?

Maybe she just hasn't listened.

Maybe if I understood why she casually gave me a mix in return comprised of . . . in the interest of kindness, I'll call them "highly suspicious" rather than "totally lame" song selections, my desire to forget this interlude of our tenuous connection could wane.

I take my doorman jacket off and place it over her shivering, goose-pimpled arms.

"I *am* going to give you shit about Bon Jovi, however," I say.

Track 4
Britney Spears: "(You Drive Me) Crazy"

"It's a great workout song!" Naomi defends. "But if you want to know why I put it on the mix, the answer is that I didn't have a lot of music to choose from. I'm just not into that stuff. Pretty much the only music I own is songs Ely liked or songs I downloaded for listening to when I go running."

There is no sigh loud enough to express my profound disappointment in Naomi.

"Gabriel." She pauses, then points her finger at me. "I will take you down if you disrespect Britney or Bon Jovi. Not because I like them that much. But cuz there's nothing wrong with them."

Nothing *wrong*. Just nothing particularly *right*.

But man, I respect the fight in her. Naomi can play tiger all over me anytime she wants.

Track 5
Dixie Chicks: "Don't Waste Your Heart"

It's probably a waste of time asking Naomi how she could even conceive of producing a mix that transitions from Britney Spears to the Dixie Chicks with no toner song in between.

She was probably thinking about Ely and not me when she chose that song.

Asking a wasted girl too much is probably a waste anyway.

Wasted girls generally turn me off—it's not the wasted part so much as the desire to *get* wasted—but this one's buzz has broken down her usual guard. Maybe that's a good thing. Girl's got issues to deal with, and better she should speak them than smoke them or, next step, snort or shoot them.

Tired and baked, she confesses, "I thought Ely would be my first. You know? Isn't that stupid? I waited for him. He never waited for me, though. Like my whole life, I couldn't keep up with him. At school, at dating. Especially at being with guys. He was always streaking ahead."

I guess I can understand how you'd want to get wasted if

the person you loved your whole life not only didn't want you but didn't wait for you.

I guess I might want to help her understand that there are better ways to deal.

Track 7
Green Day: "Poprocks & Coke"

I'm not sure I want to know how this song slipped into her mix.

Is Naomi one of those pre- or post-fans? Meaning, does she have a love of Green Day starting with their early album *Dookie*, or is she a listener who discovered them only after the twelve-year-old-girl set embraced "Boulevard of Broken Dreams"?

Naomi yawns. "I don't know. Catchy beat for a stoner song?"

"*What?*" This is sacrilege. Catchy beat, sure—but it's a song about devotion and longing and not about getting high. I sit down at the empty end of the sofa. It's tempting to place her feet on my lap and offer her a foot massage, but aside from the doorman code of what would be extremely unbecoming conduct, it's more tempting to find out how Naomi could be so musically misinformed. "What makes you think it's a stoner song?"

"*Poprocks. Coke.*"

"That's just the song title. The actual words *Poprocks* and *Coke* aren't sung once in the lyrics."

"Oh." I can never tell when Naomi looks at me if it's really attraction I sense underneath her gaze, or just disinterest. "Is it really that important?" She shuts her eyes.

Of course it's that important.

I can see the rise and fall of her breasts as she breathes underneath my jacket.

They are also important.

I want to, but I won't give up on her.

Track 8
Destiny's Child: "Bootylicious"

I don't think she's ready for my jelly, so I let her catnap. Watch her.

When she came home tonight, before she took refuge on the lobby sofa, she approached me at the doorman station. I was supposed to be watching the feed from the security monitors outside the building, but really I was watching *Court TV*. I figured Naomi would do her usual act when she appears at my doorman station—bore into the center of my soul with her eyes and then say nothing more to me than "hey" before walking away, confident (correctly) that I'd be paying close attention to the sly strut of her hips. Maybe she'd send me a suggestive text message from the elevator.

"Hey," she said, gravel-voiced. Bloodshot eyes.

I nodded and said nothing. Ready to jump up and catch her should she fall.

I expected her to walk off toward the elevator. Instead she announced, "Tonight we were going to put Robin-guy on trial for crimes against womankind, so Robin-guy said, 'Okay, but only if I can film it,' which goes to show why he needed to be on trial anyway, right? God, *so* self-absorbed. But Robin-girl—I really hope she breaks his heart, I really do—was like, 'Well, we need an impartial jury,' so I went, 'Gabriel should be the judge, because he's an archangel.' "

This is what worries me. The unoriginal associations Naomi makes with names as well as songs.

But she's thinking about me when I'm not there. Now I know that.

I like that. It dilutes the worry and replaces it with hope.

"So why didn't you come find me so I could preside?" I asked.

"Robin-guy went to find his Super 8, but he found his water bong instead and then we forgot about the trial."

My dad thinks I'm missing out on a great growing experience by not going to college, but I suspect he's mistaken.

As Naomi naps on the sofa, I take her in. She may sleep in a fetal position, but her silky hair falling over the sofa armrest and her bare legs exposed below her short skirt are damn sexy and damn well not child's play. Her sleep is anything but peaceful. She breathes unevenly and her body jerks. I imagine lying in bed next to her, stroking that hair, my leg wrapped over hers, holding her and soothing her.

She smells like marijuana smoke. It's not a bad smell. Just a sad one.

If I was her boyfriend, I'd keep her stimulated in much healthier ways.

Musically. Physically. ↱ Spiritually.

Track 11
Belle & Sebastian: "Asleep on a Sunbeam"

Mesmerized by watching Naomi asleep, I must have dozed off myself. I wake up to the sound of footsteps on the marble lobby floor.

Ely stands before us, alone. Where's the boyfriend?

As weird as it is to see Ely returning home alone, it's also a relief. It would be awkward if Naomi were to wake and see Ely. But if Bruce was standing here also—just plain painful.

It must be a song Ely liked.

It's Ely's turn now to absorb the vision of Naomi, crunched up on the sofa. Ely's eyes take in her hair, down to my doorman jacket covering her body, then on to her feet, and finally his eyes move over. To me. Next to her.

I don't know what I'm supposed to do here. It's not like I'm worried about Ely exposing me for breaking the doorman code of conduct. He'd be doing me a favor, getting me fired from this job.

It's that the silence hanging between us, the awkward

and painful glance we share, acknowledges that I'm sitting in his seat.

I start to stand up, but Ely shakes his head and gestures for me to stay seated.

"It's cool," he whispers.

I watch him stride away to the elevator.

Skip

At five-thirty, I have to wake her. I gently tap on her ankles. "Naomi," I whisper. "People are going to start coming through anytime now. You'd better get up."

She opens her eyes and smiles lazily at me. "You're a nice face to see first thing in the morning." She's still baked—content—but the guard is still down.

She's happy to see my face upon waking. That's something.

Naomi sits up, stretches her arms, then rises from the sofa. She hands me back the doorman jacket. "Thanks" is all she says. Guard rising back up. She walks off toward the elevator without a good-bye.

We can't go back to "Hey."

"Hey, Naomi," I call out after her.

She turns back around. "Yeah?"

How can I know if I'm asking too much if I never actually ask?

I stride over to the elevator. I ask:

"Did you like any of the songs on the mix I gave you?"

The elevator door opens. I step inside and beckon her in. If someone has dry cleaning to drop off—well, it can wait until I return downstairs. I hit the button for the fifteenth floor.

"I liked that Kirsty MacColl song," she says as the elevator climbs up. "I didn't know anything about her 'til I listened to that song, but I liked that song so much that I got one of her CDs."

Bingo, as the building residents like to say. If I had chosen one song on the whole playlist for her to like best, the Kirsty MacColl song would have been it.

"Which Kirsty MacColl did you buy?"

"I didn't buy it. Mom Susan 'borrowed' it for me from Ely's collection." Naomi puts her index finger to her mouth. "Shhh, don't tell. Hey, you know what? You and Mom Susan. You both like cowboy songs."

"How do you know I like cowboy songs?"

"That song with the yodeling? 'Blue Yodel'?"

Naomi really did listen to the mix I made her.

There's potential for her musical taste to improve. I feel it.

Naomi adds, almost laughing, "When you're winning Susan's quarters in those insomniac poker games in the building lobby, I feel obliged to tell you that you're taking away her secret reserve of funds for cowboy songs."

"Like what songs?" I really want Naomi to know the songs.

She shrugs. "This guy. Marty Somebody."

Close enough.

"Marty Robbins?" I ask. My father's favorite singing-in-the-shower inspiration.

"Yeah, that guy! Mom Susan used to sing us his cowboy songs when she was putting us to sleep."

"Which was your favorite song?"

"I think it was called 'Big Iron.' But when Mom Susan sang the part about *the stranger there among them had a big iron on his hip,* she'd always motion her hands like she was ironing a shirt instead of slinging a Smith & Wesson. I think I was twelve before I realized a big iron meant a gun and not an actual iron."

The elevator door opens and Naomi steps out.

I'm not going to point out that Susan put Ely and Naomi to bed when they were children like *siblings*. There was nothing for Naomi to wait for.

"Good night, Naomi," I say. I hit the button to return to the lobby. "Sweet dreams."

"Patsy Cline?" she says as the door closes between us.

FAIR

"Tonight," Ely says, "we're going to a drag version of Lilith Fair."

I have no idea what he's talking about. Except for the "drag" part. Which is enough to put me on edge.

We're in his room. He's putting on a pink shirt and a pink tie. He's putting on mascara. The closest I've ever come to wearing makeup is when my grandmothers kissed me on the cheek and left lipstick there.

"It'll be great," he goes on. "There's this one drag queen who does Aimee Mann and calls herself—well, she calls herself Aimee Man, with one *n*. And then there's Fiona Adam's-Apple and Sheryl Crowbar and Natalie Merchant-of-Penis. Pronounced so it rhymes with *Venice*. Of course."

Of course.

The truth? And I can't believe I'm thinking it, but it *is* the truth: We should be making out right now. His moms are at their book club. The apartment's all ours; it's not like my dorm room, where you can hear all the people in the hall and wonder if one of them is about to knock, like it was last night before

Ely left me to my "study sleep." I'm still tired tonight, but certainly willing. It looked promising when he kissed me hello and it lasted for fifteen minutes. Then, when it started to get grabby and unzippy, he got skittish. And while I know it's because we have plans, and I know it's because he probably spent an hour putting his outfit together, and I know it's because I'm spending the night and there will be plenty of time later, I still can't help but feel a little unsexy. I mean, I'm supposed to be the anxious, hesitant, newly gay one here, right? And then he starts talking about drag queens like they're all personal friends of his, and I feel not only unsexy, but also completely uncool. And unprepared. And inept. And insecure. Really, all it takes is one unword for all the other unwords and inwords to break through.

"It'll be fun," Ely says. This is his phrase for *c'mon, try it*. I hear it a lot, whether he's compelling me to have Indian food for the first time (verdict: fun), see a black-and-white-and-subtitled movie about the very, very, verrrrry slow breakup of a marriage (not fun), or lick whipped cream off his chest (tasty).

He's so predictable with his "It'll be fun." And I'm just as predictable, because just like every other time, I go right along.

"What's a Lilith Fair?" I ask. "It sounds like a place where lesbians run around in Renaissance costumes."

"You're not that far off," Ely tells me. "It was an all-female tour in the 1990s that Sarah McLachlan started after she was told that nobody would ever pay to see more than one female performer on the same bill. It made millions."

"Is what I'm wearing okay?" my unsexy, uncool, unprepared, inept insecurity asks.

I know that most boyfriends would shrug it off and say I look fine. Or even, on a good day, good. But the plus and minus of any transaction with Ely is the direct truth. So instead of a "Yes, dear, you're ready to go," I get a "Do you want to borrow my penguin shirt? It would look great on you."

God help me, I think he's going to give me a black shirt with a white bib, which on my body would look just about . . . penguin. But apparently, Penguin is a brand, because the shirt he gives me is five shades of green, sort of like a preppy test pattern. Green is usually a color I like, but I'm not sure about so many of them at once.

Ely chuckles. "You look scared," he says. "Let's stick with black."

I love how casual he is with his clothes. I'm an only child; I've never really worn other people's clothes. And nobody's ever really wanted to wear mine.

"When in doubt, go with black"—that's what Naomi would tell me. And now Ely's saying the same exact thing. I wonder which one learned it from the other. Or if they learned it at the same time, at the NYC Cool Kid orientation I missed.

His shirt is way too tight on me, but he doesn't seem to notice.

"I feel naked," I say. I can see the shape of my nipples.

"Here," Ely says, coming close to me with the mascara pencil, "this'll help."

I step back.

"I think I'll pass on the mascara," I say.

Ely smiles. "Eyeliner," he tells me. "Not mascara. Eyeliner."

"I like my natural lines," I say.

"I like your natural lines, too."

He makes a show of putting the pencil down, then comes over and wraps his arms around me.

"Close your eyes," he says.

"What are you going to do to me?" I ask. Maybe he has some lipstick in his pocket.

"Nothing," he says. "Trust me."

I close my eyes. I feel him stepping back. Then I feel closeness again. A little brushing on my cheeks.

Eyelashes. His eyelashes. Working their way to mine.

"Be careful," he whispers. "I might rub off on you."

And I whisper, "Bollocks."

The Lilith Fair is on the Lower East Side, at a club that I'm not sure I can get into.

"I don't have an ID," I remind Ely.

"If the doorman gives you trouble, I'll just show him my dick," Ely replies.

I don't feel much better.

I feel even worse when we get there and find a line full of

hipless hipsters, drag queens holding court, go-go boy aspirants, and flavas of the week.

"I guess word got out," Ely mumbles.

It's almost sweet to see Ely in a crowd that's never heard of him. It means he has to wait on line like everyone else.

"This one time?" Ely says, and I almost expect him to continue with *"At band camp?"* But instead he says the quarantined name—"Naomi and I decided to go to the Night of a Thousand Stevies. Just to see all the girls and guys dressed like Stevie Nicks. And Naomi? She thought it would be really funny if she went as Stevie Wonder. This one drag queen nearly suffocated her in muslin. It was a time."

He's not only said her name, but he's tied it to a good memory. It makes me hopeful, but I don't want to jinx it by pointing it out.

The line is moving slowly, and some people who were ahead of us are actually walking back the way they came—meaning: The bouncer is actually bouncing.

There is no way I'm going to make the cut.

I don't know this as an objective fact; I've never actually been bounced in my entire life, for the simple reason that I've never put myself in a position where there was any risk of being bounced. I mean, you can get through life pretty easily if you avoid places guarded by bouncers. It's not like they're at supermarkets or libraries.

"What's the name of this place, anyway?" I ask.

"I dunno," Ely replies. "It changes every night."

Odds are the name's a pretentious singular noun—bouncered hipster establishments are usually named with a pretentious singular noun. Not unlike perfumes. *I put on a little Enchantress in order to go downtown to Fugue.* Or *I sprayed my wrist with some Mannerism, and we hopped from Heathen to Backwash to Striation and then ended the night at End.*

Personally, if I ever open a club, I'm naming it Inquisition.

The bouncer tonight is certainly a sight I've never seen in econ class. It's this ginormous guy dressed in what looks like an inflatable pouch of parachute fabric. Ely laughs when he sees the guy, but it's a joke I don't get. Which is made even worse when we get to the front of the line and the bouncer looks at me and asks, "Who am I?"

I'm stuck on *Do I know you?* when Ely jumps in and says, "You're Missy Elliot! Lilith Fair's token black girl from year two!"

This is clearly the right answer, but the bouncer isn't about to give me the prize.

"I wasn't asking you," he says to Ely. "Now you get to go in, but he stays out."

This is nothing short of humiliating. I know Ely's getting in because he's hot, and I'm being bounced because I'm not—musical trivia aside.

"C'mon . . . pleeeeeeease?" Ely says, batting his eyelashes.

The bouncer shakes his head and starts to look at the guy behind me, who has done his hair in braids.

"I'll show you my dick!" Ely playfully offers.

This makes the bouncer smile and raise his eyebrow.

"Here," Ely says, and before I can stop him, he's unbuttoned his fly and pulled out the waistband of his underwear so the bouncer can take a look.

"Not bad," the bouncer says to Ely. "You're a lucky guy." Then he looks at me and says, "You are, too."

As I walk by, the bouncer spanks me on the ass.

I am so not in the mood.

Ely's beaming, like the winning contestant on a reality show.

"You really didn't have to do that," I have to say.

"No worries. All in a day's work."

And I guess what I should've said is: *You really shouldn't have done that.* Not that there's anything wrong with what he did—it's his dick, and he can show it to whoever he wants. In passing. But it's like he's given me a new definition of himself for me to consider and feel inadequate about. I am not the kind of guy who has a boyfriend who shows his dick to a stranger. I know this. And he has just proved himself to be a guy who shows his dick to a stranger. *And he's not even drunk.*

Therefore.

Ergo.

Erg.

Argh.

Ugh.

We're on completely different tracks now, our evening splitting in two directions. His is up. Mine is down. The club is packed, and the DJ is blasting beat-heavy remixes of ordinarily mellow Liliths. Ely's loving it, *loving it*— I know this because he's calling out, "I'm loving this—*loving this*!" He gets a Fiona Appletini at the bar, and I get one, too, but for a different reason—his is to enhance and mine is to deny.

My boyfriend's a hit. Other boys are coming over to flirt. Some are clearly repeat flirters, and Ely clearly doesn't remember any of their names. As he talks to them, he holds my hand. Ordinarily this would make me feel giddy with mine-mine-mine-ness, but now I feel like I should say to him, *Oh no no no, don't mind me, you go ahead and have a good time. I'll just go home and watch PBS.*

It's funny, because I think about how Naomi must've known what this was like. Although she, at least, could hold her own. My version of flirting bears a striking resemblance to mime.

I want to pull Ely aside and ask *Who are you?* And *Why haven't we had sex yet?* (Slept together? Yes. First, second, and third bases? Covered. All the way? Nope.) And *Why are you with me?* But I am so terrified of sounding needy. And I am so resentful that there is no *want* version of the word *needy*— *And that was the point where he got all wanty on me. "I'm sorry," I said, "but you have some serious wantiness issues."* And maybe I *do* have wantiness issues. I want to go. I want to be alone with him. I want to be the kind of person who has a boyfriend who shows his dick to a stranger—once, in order to get them into a club. I want to be cool enough. I want to erase all these thoughts—all thoughts, period—and have a good time. But Ely can't just show his dick to my wantiness and make it go away.

I feel like the mutant among the mutants. Like the boy who showed up at Xavier's School for Gifted Youngsters and found out that, whoops, he didn't have any superpowers at all.

I'm so tired of being uncool. You can dress me up, give me a cool boyfriend, even laugh at one of my jokes every now and then—but the anxiety always gives it away.

The techno Lilith ends and the floor show begins. The hostess is a drag queen calling herself Sarah McLocklips, and she starts by asking for some volunteers from the audience to be the impromptu opening act—apparently, Paula Cole-Minor's-Slaughter retired and nobody bothered to tell the organizers. The music's all cued—they just need a Paula.

Before you can say "Where have all the cowboys gone?" Ely's onstage.

"Because my friend Naomi has all five seasons of *Dawson's Creek*, I think I know this one cold," he says. Then, warming into it, he adds, "This one is for Pacey, for being the Jughead. And Jen, who never got the respect she deserved. And Bruce."

("Was Bruce the gay one?" the girl next to me asks her staple-pierced boyfriend.

"No, that was Jack," the punk replies. "Andie's brother."

"Oh! I loved Andie!" the girl screams.)

Ely doesn't even try to sound like Paula Cole—instead he belts the song out like it's graduation.

> *I don't want to wait*
> *For our lives to be over . . .*

Since neither Pacey nor Jen is in the room, he's looking at me as he sings it. So I smile and cheer and sing along when he asks everyone to join him. But what I'm thinking is: *I don't want to wait, either. And I don't want you to have to wait.*

Everyone adores him. What can I give him besides that, besides what everyone else does?

When the song ends, he's more popular than ever. People buy him drinks. He puts his hand on their shoulders as he says thank you. It's not an invitation; he's just being nice. He'd hold my hand if I offered it. But I'm off offering. I don't just feel like the third wheel—it's more like the twenty-sixth.

I don't blame him. I direct it all at myself. For not being able to go along.

I finally make my excuses and shove my way to the restroom. The person in front of me is clearly Natalie Merchant-of-Penis, since her T-shirt reads I BLEW 10,000 MANIACS AND ALL I GOT WAS THIS STUPID T-SHIRT. She takes so long inside that I'm worried she's found her 10,001st maniac, but when she emerges, she's all alone. When she passes me, she says, "I just want to thank you," and I don't know what to do but nod.

Once I've locked the door behind me, I do my business. And then I just sit there, because I realize I don't want to face Ely yet. In fact, I realize that I'm actually going to leave. And I'm not even going to tell Ely I'm leaving, since I don't want to ruin his night. I want him to stay and have fun. I'll text him once I'm safely away. I don't want to rain on his parade. Although, yeah, I wouldn't mind if his parade decided to follow me out the door.

I look at all the graffiti in the stall. Some of it even has pictures. I don't understand half of it. It's only after I've been reading for two minutes or so and the person waiting outside has started to pound on the door that I know what I've been looking for—not words of wisdom, but a blank space.

There's one available under an inscription that says:

The Cure. For the Ex's? I'm sorry, Nick. You know. Will you kiss me again?

I take a pen out of my pocket and write:

Ely, I want. You, me, the rest of it. I want someone to make it work, and I don't know if it can be me. Because I'm so uncool and so afraid.

I wonder if you're supposed to sign something like this. But I figure if he ever sees it, he'll know it's from me. And if he doesn't know it's from me . . . well, then it wasn't meant to happen anyway.

When I leave the bathroom, the person waiting says pretty much the opposite of "I just want to thank you." But that's the least of my cares. I search the club for Ely, thinking maybe I'll say good-bye in person after all. But then I see him at the bar, drinking his bright green drink and chatting with the bouncer from before and two gay boys who almost look like they could be twins. They're all laughing. Enjoying themselves.

I feel like an outsider to that. To Ely, and to that. So I head where the outsiders belong: outside.

I'm never going to fit in with him. Never.

I know this is the wrong choice. But it feels like the only choice. So I make it.

UP

Was that you I just heard snort from the other side of class?

I didn't realize the sound of a snort could carry as far as where girl-Robin, sitting on the opposite end of the lecture hall, is IM'ing me during Introduction to Psychology class. At least I didn't fart.

Yeah, I type back. *Bruce the First's new thing is to e-mail me daily inspirational quotes.* I copy and paste today's installment into the IM screen and send it over to Robin. *"And I've learned what is obvious to a child. That life is simply a collection of little lives, each lived one day at a time. That each day should be spent finding beauty in flowers and poetry and talking to animals. That a day spent with dreaming and sunsets and refreshing breezes cannot be bettered. But most of all, I learned that life is about sitting on benches next to ancient creeks with my hand on her knee and sometimes, on a good day, for falling in love." —Nicholas Sparks*

Robin's hearty snort from the other side of the room is twice as loud as mine. Schenectady really knows how to raise 'em right.

Here's the math on psych: Probably one hundred students in this class. Eighty percent type lecture notes into their laptops as the professor-drone pontificates about some sick experiment where people were told to perform a task completely unrelated to the behavior they were actually being observed for (shrinks are mean fucks but excellent liars—I respect that). The remaining 20 percent of students appear to be dozing, while easily half the laptop note takers are IM'ing or perusing online dating services instead of paying attention to professor-drone. The likelihood that I will fail this class is about 60/40 (professor-drone's T.A. has a thing for me, but I can't bother to fake a girl-crush on her, even for a passing grade). I'm here, though. The odds of me bothering to show at any class these days are nil.

But I had to escape Mom. She took another sick day off work. Since I wouldn't have the apartment to myself, where I could spend the day not being in class, and I couldn't bear a third consecutive day of hanging out in Mom's giant bed reading fashion mags and watching DVDs while she naps, I opted to go to class. But I arrived too late to grab a seat by Robin, dutifully sitting in the front row.

She queries:

☺ *I thought Bruce the First was over you.*

I respond:

I think he is. But he will never get over Nicholas Sparks. ☺

This time our laughs are in sync. Only mine is louder, and the professor has to stop lecturing to point up at me. "You in the back? Do you have something you care to share with the class? Or are experiments in human reaction to animal torture really that funny?"

A hundred faces turn to me. "Sorry," I mumble.

I lied. I'm not sorry.

I totally want to stand up and leave. Just like that. Leave this class and leave this university. For good.

Only I have nothing to go to. No one to help me along the way.

Ely.

It's like I can smell him.

I *did* want to escape this lecture room, but then I see him through the glass windows in the door at the front of the room, walking through the hallway with a group of gay boys, easily identifiable as such by too much hair gel and clothing choices that are too carefully mismatched, and I'm fine to stay through the end of class. No Bruce the Second in sight. Must be Queer Boys With Assumed Musical Superiority Who Recycle For A Greener Rainbow Environment meeting day.

Then: *Ouch.*

I know Robin means the Ely sighting and not the professor's interruption.

They travel in packs, you know, I answer.

Who?

😎 *Gay boys* 😎.

It's true. I wasted my time creating rules for Ely and me to avoid each other in The Building when where I've really needed to avoid him is Everywhere Else. There he is, standing in line at the Mud-coffee truck in front of the Virgin store in Union Square, about to kiss Bruce the Second. Or I see him at six in the morning, sitting in the window seat at the twenty-four-hour Ukrainian restaurant across the street from the Starbucks on Second Avenue and East Ninth, where I've taken up new residence solely to avoid Ely sightings; he's dining with a posse of gay boys after what must be a late night out, wearing *my* pink shirt and compulsively glancing at his cell phone every two minutes even though he *knows* there's no text message from me. It's not The Building that's too small for us anymore—it's the whole damn city below Fourteenth Street.

I wish my vision lied, but what I see is that Ely looks happier with him, with them, than he ever did with me. He's more comfortable, relaxed—like he's sacrificed a crucial element in his life but won back the elemental right not to have to worry about a bomb randomly and unexpectedly going off in his midst. He probably prefers being surrounded by his own kind. Not every gay boy needs to accessorize with a straight-girl best friend. *That* is the lie.

Robin asks, *What about Gabriel?*

He asked me to Starbucks.

That's big. Did you go?

Not yet. But I'm thinking 'bout it.

Good. If Bruce the First can move on, so can you.

I'm a little awed that Robin can IM so rapidly when I

know she is also typing lecture notes. I admire multi-taskers. I decide to follow her lead. I open a new document on my laptop.

THINGS BETTER EXPERIENCED WITHOUT ELY

1. Bingo.

Ely totally messed with my juju. I never won when I played with him sitting at my side, but since we've worked out an alternating-Tuesdays schedule for bingo playing, I've discovered a lucky winning streak. Who knew? The old people in The Building touch me for luck when I pass by them now, I swear.

2. Frappuccinos.

The tasty treats Ely hates. Yummmmmmmmmmm.

3. *Dawson's Creek.*

Ely's a Dawson-Joey 'shipper (and I don't think that's because Dawson was *so clearly gay;* I think Ely really believed that girl-next-door Joey was Dawson's true love), whereas I am all about the Pacey-Joey true love, and debating the issue with Ely is useless when the final episode proves me *so clearly right.*

4. Love Thyself.

Okay, I've given up on *Seventeen* entirely (some things are sacred), but even reading *Cosmo* without Ely is not the same fun, and defacing the models with our crayon collection is rather pointless without him (Ely draws a dick much better than I). But *Cosmo* does have a point: Thinking about someone you're really really attracted to while touching yourself can yield satisfactory—*very* satisfactory—results. And when I think about Gabriel touching me here-there-everywhere while I'm doing just that, I seem to reach a place I never found when fantasizing about doing it with Ely. It makes me want to find that place for real with a real person—a person named Gabriel and not named Ely.

Oh. My. God. No wonder I don't go to class. The professor has decided to run a slide show sponsored by PETA, apparently. I can't look. I don't want Robin to look. So I distract her with a new IM:

What does sex feel like?

She turns around so I can see her face looking up at me. Her jaw drops. Then she types back:

Are you serious? You've never done it?!?!? YOU?!?!?

I shrug, then send: ☻. I *almost* did it with Bruce the Second. But I knew we were both going through motions to express a feeling we didn't actually feel for one another, and he seemed to know the same, and he never pushed it like most guys. And I don't think that's because Bruce the Second is *so clearly probably gay.* I think maybe it's because he's just a good guy.

I hate that.

I guess I hope he finds what he's looking for. Bruce the Second, that is.

Robin responds:

People say you should wait to be with someone you love, but I think it's more important to be with someone you like. I mean, that person is going to see you naked, you know? Be inside you. Don't do it for the sake of doing it, but don't wait for a fantasy, either.

Friends? I type back.

She turns around again, smiles up at me.

Yeah. ☺

And suddenly I want to fall out of my chair with ☺ laughter ☺. Because I am imagining Ely on top of me, naked, penetrating me, and the mental image is *so clearly wrong.* The intimacy may be loving, the intentions are good, he's up and in me, but it's awkward and forced—worse than the deadening image of watching porn, because the *feeling* part of the chemical components between us just could not be right. Naomi + Ely should not = sex.

Ely likes boys. I like boys. Ely is a boy. I am a girl.

📱 *Ring* 📱 *ring,* Naomi. How can you even be in college when you're so dumb as to take this long to make the connection? To truly believe it?

It's not funny, so I don't know why I am laughing so hard. But my dream vision, which won't lie to me even as fantasy, is just that ridiculous.

I will never understand why gender is so important to mating rituals—it doesn't make sense; love is love, attraction is what it is, and why should the arbitrary assignment of genital parts determine whether or not you want to be with a person?—but the fact is, it matters.

I hate that, too.

But it's true.

And if I'm going to face the cold, hard truth, someone else should, too.

I'm out of here, I type to Robin.

Are you leaving in the middle of the class? Where are you going?

Home.

Mourning has to end. For both of us.

Time to get Mom up and out of bed.

EASY

After a few days of awkwardness and avoidance with Bruce, I call an emergency meeting of the Dairy Queens. With Naomi and Bruce out of range, I need to call in the backup support system. I figure if you're facing big dilemmas or difficult personal problems, it always helps to get the perspective of a few gay boys who grew up in farm country. The shit they had to deal with makes mine look puny. And to survive in style . . . well, we could all learn a lot from that.

We meet right after class. Shaun (linebacker from Nebraska) is wearing his usual rugby shirt and jeans; I used to dismiss him as "straight-acting" until I realized that he was just acting like himself, and that playing the "straight-acting" card was just a weird way for gay boys to hate themselves and each other. Art (from Idaho) is wearing an XXS T-shirt that's embroidered with the phrase I AIN'T YOUR BITCH. Neal (our F2M transitioning pal from southern Illinois) is sexy as hell in a British-schoolboy-with-his-striped-tie-all-askew ensemble, and Ink (who had such a miserable time in Missouri that his first tattoo said GET ME OUT OF HERE across the inside of his arm) is his usual mess of plaids and blacks. It's been a while since I've needed them like this, and they're good enough to me not to mention that.

As we're heading out, we pass Naomi's psych class. I always learned her schedules before I learned my own, and I feel nostalgic for that now. But I can't invite her along, not right now—I have to deal with my life one failure at a time, because if I consider them all at once, I might fall into a bucketless well.

I'm not the only one with problems. As we walk past Washington Square Park (too many people we know, too much social noise) and down to the Hudson, Ink talks about how he tried to call his mother for her birthday only to have her refuse to come to the phone, no matter how hard his sisters tried to persuade her. Art then recounts a sadistic night out—"sadistic in the bad way"—with a Facebook date who ended up being forty pounds heavier, six years older, and five blank hours duller than he'd been when they were e-mailing. And Neal says his ex has started calling again, making booty overtures and nearly wrecking his latest like.

Shaun stays silent about himself, and I wonder if it's because I'm there. Even though I dated Ink for a week during freshman orientation and once made out with Neal at a party, Shaun's the one who didn't appear on the No Kiss List until it was too late. I flirted recklessly and it nearly wrecked everything.

We walk 'til we get to Rockefeller Park, right on the river.

As soon as we hit the grass, Neal asks me what's going on, and if I've heard from Bruce yet.

It's a simple question, and my answer takes about twenty minutes. I start with the night Bruce disappeared, because even though Neal and Art were there, Shaun and Ink weren't. I talk about how confused I was, and how I'm still just as confused, if not more so. I admit: I should have clued in earlier that Bruce had disappeared. At first I thought there was just a really long line for the boys' room, because a lot of the time, there is. Then I figured he'd found other friends to talk to or something. It was only after he'd been gone for about an hour that I noticed, wow, it had been an hour. I confess I even thought, *Oh shit, now I'm going to get in trouble for leaving him alone for an hour.* It never occurred to me that he might have left without saying good-bye. I looked everywhere for him and enlisted Neal and Art to look, too. I asked the people on the bathroom line if they'd seen someone fitting Bruce's description, but they assured me the only person in the bathroom at that moment was a Jewel-inspired drag queen (Family Jewel). Finally I bumped into the Missy Elliot bouncer, who told me my fly guy had flown. I checked my voice mail and texts: nothing. I even had Neal text me and Art call me, just to make sure the phone was working. I tried calling Bruce. No answer. I texted him: *Where are you? Are you okay?*

Finally, about ten minutes later, I received a text back from him:

I'm safe and sound. Have a good night.

That was it. No apology. No explanation.

Which was so not like him. It was, in fact, more like me. To be so careless.

I texted him again, asking what was going on. Neal, Art, and I left the club and headed to a diner for a three-in-the-morning three-stack of pancakes. We found a larger gay-boy contingent there and pulled up chairs to join them. I was totally in my scene: all the flirty banter, all the caustic observation, all the naked desire for affection . . . this was a game I played well. But instead of playing, I spent the whole time looking at my phone, waiting for him to text back. With other boys, I would have just called back and left a fuck-you message on their voice mail. But the point of Bruce is that he isn't one of those other boys. He's Bruce.

Now it's four days later, and we've only had two conversations, both of them rushed, neither of them satisfying. I tell the Dairy Queens that he said he wants to *figure things out*. He apologized a lot for leaving, but he hasn't made any effort to come back.

"This isn't good," Neal says, shaking his head. "This is like an orange alert, breakup-wise."

"And orange is such a *difficult* color," Art adds.

I am too conscious of having Shaun here. He's a reminder of everything I've done wrong before. It became, for me, a pattern as common as plaid: I'd throw myself on someone, then throw him out. Shaun was different from most of the rest, because he'd actually thrown my actions back at me, yelling and crying as I dumped him, telling me that I was going to end up graduating NYU with a major in Fuck & Run. Because that's what I was: an F&R boy. Shaun had seen me do it to other guys, which made him feel even more stupid when I did it to him . . . and made me feel even worse. Like I should have known. But the hardest thing was that I always believed in it at first—I never F'd with the intention of R-ing. But in the end—when we got to the end—the boys never believed this. Only Naomi did, really. After Shaun had it out with me, I went straight to her, sobbing. "It hurts to hurt people when you never mean to, doesn't it?" she'd asked. And I'd said yes. It really, really hurt. When it was casual, when everything was understood ahead of time, it was fine. But when you really wanted it to work, when you really thought it could become something—well, then the F was never worth the R.

But Bruce was supposed to be different. With Bruce, I tried to be more careful. I tried to trick the pattern. I decided that if we didn't jump to the F stage, then I wouldn't jump to the R stage. I tried to slow things down—*which is not an easy thing for me to do.* And I found that slowing down the sex thing actually quickened the heart thing. It was like I'd set up this test, and I was passing it for a reason: I liked him. A lot. The sexual attraction was still there—I wasn't so deluded as to think I could hold out for someone *ugly*—but I tried to focus on all the other attractions. To his goofiness. To his goodness. To his *sincerity.* It made me want to be attractive in those ways, too.

We didn't F; I didn't R. I was doing everything right.

And then he was the one who ran.

I can't say all of this to the DQs, not with Shaun right

there, because I know we're still at the stage where he hears himself in anything I say about boyfriends. So I don't talk about before and what I was like before.

Instead I say, "I tried. I really tried. And it's so frustrating that none of that matters."

"You did try," Neal says, trying to comfort me.

"You did," Art echoes.

And it's Shaun who says, "So don't stop trying now."

There's a remnant of anger in his voice, and I think, *Yes, I deserve that—I really deserve that.* But I realize he's not as angry at me for what I did to him as he is annoyed at the fact that it seems I'm wussing out.

It's like Naomi's talking to me, calling me on it.

"Listen," she and Shaun say. "You're giving up. You're slipping into being miserable, because if you're miserable, then it's all about you again. But it's not all about you. Love doesn't work that way."

Neal looks at me with sympathy in his eyes. "You didn't think it would be easy, did you?" he asks. "You didn't think there was a way that you could be so fabulous and so fantastic and so perfect that it would actually be easy? It's never easy for anyone. Don't you know that?"

I don't know why this gets to me. Because, yes, I guess there was a part of me that thought it could be easy. That something that is worth so much could just be given to you. Because you were cute. Or sexy. Or on your best behavior. It can sometimes make it easier, but it can never make it easy. I thought when I found the right person, it would be easy. He would be mine and I would be his and that would be that. And with Naomi. I would be hers and she would be mine and that would be that. The perfect friendship. The ideal. What kind of tension could a straight girl and a gay boy have? None. Easy.

No. No no no no. It is not easy. Things that matter are not easy. Feelings of happiness are easy. Happiness is not. Flirting is easy. Love is not. Saying you're friends is easy. Being friends is not.

"Ely?" Neal asks. I haven't answered his question yet; instead I've started laughing at myself. For being so foolish. For not getting it.

"I'm sorry," I say, not wanting the DQs to think I'm laughing at them. "It's just that . . . I really *did* think it could be easy. For me."

At this, Neal leans over and puts his arms around my shoulders. Ink laughs along at me. Shaun gives me a look that says, *Yes, you are a stupid one, aren't you?* Art just pats my leg, like I've learned a new trick.

I get it now. I swear, I get it. And it's like this was the thing I needed to know in order to make all the other things I knew make sense.

It's funny how much easier it makes it, to know that it's not going to be easy.

"I'm sorry," I say. "I'm sorry."

I'm saying it to all of them. But really, I'm saying it most to Shaun. To Bruce. To Naomi. Not because I think it's all my fault—I know it's not all my fault. I guess *I'm sorry* is a way to say *I want it to be better.* Even if it's difficult. Even if it hurts.

I have to stop hiding behind who I am. I have to stop hiding behind the things other people expect from me and the things I expect from myself. I have to try.

I tell this to the Dairy Queens. I tell them I have to figure out where to start.

And then I say, "Any suggestions?"

EXPECTATION

Naomi Ely

Living a life separate from Ely across the hall is easy. It hasn't been fun, certainly—but it's completely doable. We can break out physical territories just fine. The last six weeks, give or take a few misdemeanor encounters, have proved that.

I guess I can let go of Ely after all. It's letting go of the future mental expectation for Naomi & Ely that feels impossible. No, *impossible* is the wrong word. I know it's possible. We're living apart already. *Unfair* is what it is. The one fantasy that's comforted me through my life so far, that's given me a reason to go on and to hope for my—for *our*—future, is just that: **F-A-N-T-A-S-Y**.

Ely and I would finish college, get married, buy a 🏠 and a 🚗, and have a 👶. We'd be a family just like a 👪, totally ignoring the impossible obstacles right in front of us. *La-la-la,* Ely is queer; *la-la-la* and *ha-ha-ha,* Naomi fell into that tired old trap of loving someone who could never love her back the same way. Naomi & Ely just stuck with the same old program because it's what expectation told them to do. Joke's on them, *fools*.

It must be expectation that Mom can't let go of, either. I mean, I don't think she expects Dad to waltz back into our apartment and everything to be all right again. We wouldn't have him back even if he wanted to come back. Yet we still live in this apartment, where all the hurtful memories exist not as ghosts but as neighbors. It's not fantasy or mirage: *They're there*. The photos of Dad with us as a family still linger on our tables and walls, his clothes still hang in a closet we don't dare open, his mail even still comes here. It's like he left and time just stopped. We continued on, but only because we had to. The apartment's shell remained the same (less that small section of the living room wall Mom destroyed back when she was feeling the pain rather than numbing it), but the inside we can't see, the emptiness we don't acknowledge—because how could we; the physical props of Dad's presence still exist, *right in front of us*—have eaten us alive.

It's as if Mom somehow expects a magic potion will come along and fix this lie we're living in; 'til then, she'll sleep.

I wake her by spraying Evian spritz onto her face. This method is not only gentle, but good for our shared milky-smooth complexion. Every magazine says so.

Her eyes pop open and the hazel-eyed look of simultaneous anger and love she flashes me reminds me how much Mom and I look alike. Ely always envied me that I could look at my mom and know exactly where I came from. He doesn't look like anyone in his known family. I always liked that this face I share with Mom was worthy of Ely's envy. Yet, as with all things, he bested me in the envy contest, too. Maybe he got the mystery face, but he also got the functional family, the one that survived and worked things out instead of just falling apart. The family that can survive and then thrive is so much more worthy of envy, in my opinion. That's *work*. A beautiful face passed down from a mother? That's just a gift.

"What are you doing, Naomi?" Mom murmurs. She closes her eyes again and turns over, away from me. "If you're not here to watch *Oprah,* then go away."

I jump over to the other side of the bed. And spray again, a direct shot onto her face, then her hair, her arms, her . . .

"NAOMI! What are you DOING?"

She's furious, but I smile at her, cuddle into her. There's no need for shouting. "Wake up, Mom," I murmur back.

She pulls me to her, tight. "I'm up," she whispers into my ear. Then she grabs the Evian bottle and takes a turn to spray my face.

"That feels nice," I say. "Refreshing."

"Naomi."

"Right."

"Naomi, what are you doing?" Mom doesn't wait for my answer. She reaches for the TV remote. I grab it from her hands before Oprah can overtake my efforts to get Mom out of bed to deal with her own problems rather than tune in for Oprah to fix everybody else's.

I stand up on the bed and jump up and down, up and down. "GET UP GET UP GET UP!" I sing these words, but it's not until the chant is over that I make the connection of what I just did, the Sunday-morning make-us-breakfast rou-tine I just replayed.

"Ely," Mom says. "Isn't he supposed to be here double-teaming if you're going to pull this act?"

She's got me there. He should be here.

"We have to move," I tell her.

"What? You're crazy. Don't you have homework to do, or something?"

"He's not coming back."

Silence.

She knows I'm not talking about Ely.

Then:

"I know," she acknowledges.

"You wouldn't want him to come back even if he did."

"I know that, too."

"So why are you still in bed?" *His* bed. *Their* bed.

Mom doesn't stand up, but she at least sits up. But it's like the view from Awake is too bright. She places her head down into her hands. "I don't know, honey. I just don't know. I don't know what else to do. I hate my job. I can't afford for us to move. I feel trapped."

"Then let's change the mental expectation. Let's not think of being trapped. Let's think of our situation as . . . a maze we have to find our way out of. The thing about a trap is you get caught and can't get out. A maze has an exit. You just have to find it."

"And how do we do that, O abruptly wizened daughter?"

"We can start by selling this apartment and moving, Mommy."

Her head pops up to throw a Naomi brand of stare-glare face at me. "It needs to be fixed up in order to get it on the market. There's the damage in the living room. The kitchen and bathroom need to be retiled. The blinds are falling apart. The list called Impossible goes on and on."

"We can get help."

"Are you listening, Naomi? I HAVE NO MONEY."

"But you have options. We could ask Grandma to help. She has lots of money."

"She's too controlling. There's always a price to be paid for her quote-unquote 'help.' "

"So what? Pay that price. Visit her every couple of months. Let her tell you to get a divorce and get back into circulation. Say thank you when she offers up completely bad career advice."

Mom laughs. It's a start.

I watch her my-face churning in thought. Then she sparks. "Maybe we could ask Gabriel if he's interested in taking on a side job—help out with some of the work that needs to be done on the apartment? He's a nice guy, huh? Maybe he'd help out, and we'd get a chance to get to know him at the same time?" She appears serious, but her voice teases. "You *liiiiike* him."

I love my mom.

"Maybe," I allow.

My real challenge is to figure out how the hell we find a Realtor willing not only to take on this falling-apart apartment but its falling-apart mother-daughter sellers. "Guess what?" I say.

"That's what!" Mom answers.

"I'm kind of failing out of school and should probably just drop out."

Mom's head falls back into her hands. "Oh Lord," she sighs. Her head's bounce back upward to look at me is surprisingly quick in response—and no glare this time, either. "I knew it was coming. Not this, exactly—but something like this. Your teenage years were too easy. Just tell me now, get it over with. You're not pregnant or doing drugs, are you?"

She's right. I did go easy on her in my high school years. Yes, I had my moods. Every teenager does. Especially me. I could earn a degree in moodiness. I'd pass that course of study with all honors. But I wasn't raging teen rebellion, either. Mom was such a wronged party then. Just not by me. I didn't want to add to her pain.

Ely bested me in the teen rebellion contest, too. He totally acted out with Ginny when all that horrific shit was going down with our parents. He was *awful* to her, but protective and kind with Susan—a Jekyll-and-Hyde personality with his own parents. And now, if he's allowed to have boys spend the night, or if he stays out all night with no recrimination from them, it's not because he's reached college age or they're too passed out to notice. It's because of the precedent he set—no, that he *demanded*—when he was still in high school. That freedom he won too soon was the price his parents paid for the mess the collective parents made. Grew him up too soon. Grew both of us up too soon, I guess; we just acted it out in different ways. Ely turned promiscuous. I chose fantasy.

His promiscuity that I can no longer choose to tune out probably has a lot to do with why Ely plays with so many boys . . . yet none have turned out to be keepers. That is, until he stole my boyfriend. Woke me up.

"I'm not pregnant," I acknowledge to Mom.

"Shit," she mutters. But at last she stands up. She's out of bed.

"What are you doing?" I ask her.

She reaches for the phone. "We *both* need help."

Here's the **?** I would ask a potential therapist: Can we live without the fantasy and still expect a fair and happy path? There's no pill for that, is there. (Not a question.)

Mom wouldn't take Dad back. But it's true. I would— *should*—take Ely back.

He didn't do anything wrong other than be who he is.

I love who Ely is.

I hate that I probably owe Ely asking him back rather than waiting for him to make the first move, for him to fix it for me, like he always has in the past. But I haven't reached that part of the maze yet. One step at a time.

I may have gotten Mom out of bed and into action, but as for:

Naomi Ely

I still don't see the way out.

But I don't feel like we're trapped, either.

CORNER

I wait for her in the stairwell off of floor six. Our hallowed ground. Suburban kids had the deluxe tree houses; we lived in Manhattan, so we had to create our own spaces. The corner of the floor six stairwell was ours. We liked the overhead strobe lighting, all flickery and buzzing. We played endless games of Sorry!, Rummikub, Apples to Apples, and our own version of Trivial Pursuit, where we'd use the board but make up our own categories and questions, usually about the other building residents. We even hung our school artwork up on the stairwell walls. When we were in middle school, the stairwell served as a stage when we played disco musical. I built the sets and she named our characters—she was Lavender and I was Butterscotch. (That memory can definitely be stuffed into the Repression Closet. I mean, the disco part was awesome, but *Butterscotch*? I let that bossy bitch call me *Butterscotch*?) Later, we took sanctuary here when our parents fought. And we wrote our first No Kiss Lists here, memorizing them before they were destroyed.

I officially came out to her at the very spot where I'm

standing now. We were fifteen, and I told her even though we both already knew. I deliberately chose the very place where we'd once carved our names into the wall.

I'm looking at it now. The imprint we scratched when we were twelve still remains:

> Naomi + Ely
> 2gether
> <u>+ 4ever</u>
> = 6ess.

There's no way for me to know she'll find me here. I didn't call. I didn't text. I left it up to that old connection, that old friendship sense.

It's like Naomi always used to say: *Life tells you to take the elevator, but love tells you to take the stairs.*

I'm counting on that. And I've been counting on it for almost an hour now.

I'm about to give up, but I stop. I always try to last at least three minutes longer than giving up.

I'm here, Naomi. I'm here.

The door opens, and I hear the clomp of her Docs. Even harder than resisting the impulse to give up is resisting the impulse to run.

The fact that you think of yourself as a runner is what makes you run. Stop that.

Now: moment of truth. She sounds like she's reached about floor eight, coming down . . . DOWN . . . and . . .

The Docs stop. She notices me.

And I notice her. I notice something's happened. I notice she's as beautiful as ever, but that she hasn't put any thought into it. I notice she needs sleep and conversation and a kiss from someone who isn't me. I notice she's still angry at me but that there are other emotions there as well. I notice her the way you notice the differences in someone who's been away a long time. And it hasn't been a long time. It's only been long for us.

It's not easy, I remind myself. *It's not easy for any of us.*

"Hi," I say.

"Hi," she says.

This, especially, isn't easy.

I look at the Naomi + Ely equation on the wall. I want to think we still add up.

I will not be intimidated by the differences between now and then. I know the blue comfort sweater she's wearing, and I know who she broke up with the day she bought those jeans, and I was the one who convinced her to buy those Docs, which look even better now that they're scratched and worn. Now all I need to do is take all of this history, all these associations, and turn them from a tense present into a present tense.

This is our corner. We're inside the force field. Nothing can hurt us.

"I think we should get married *here*," I say. It's so obvious.

Naomi sits down on the top stair, the edge of our corner, and rests her head against the wall. "Ely," she says, "we're never getting married. *Never.*"

She says it as if it's some kind of revelation. Some kind of decision. But I've known this ever since I knew I wanted to be with guys. The only thing that's a surprise to me is that it could have been a surprise to her.

"Oh, Naomi . . . ," I say, sitting down next to her, leaning close.

She doesn't lean back into me, but she doesn't stiffen up, either.

"I'm so tired, Ely," she tells me. "I don't have the energy to be fighting you."

"I never wanted to fight," I say. "I never wanted any of this."

I know what she's thinking. *If you never wanted any of this, why did you kiss Bruce the Second?* I'll plead guilty if I need to, but I won't feel guilty. Even though it was the wrong start, I know it's the right thing. For all of us.

And I guess I'm not the only mind reader in this dynamic duo, because now Naomi says, "Wouldn't it just figure that the one time you're monogamous and in love, it would be with my boyfriend?"

"Well, if it's any consolation, I probably screwed that up, too." It hurts now that she hasn't even been around to see it. To let me share it with her.

"Holy shit," she says.

"What?"

"I said 'monogamous and in love' and you didn't argue with me. You didn't tell me to fuck off."

"So?"

"*So* . . . that means it's true. Wow."

"Is that okay?" I ask cautiously. "Am I allowed to be in love?"

This would be the time for Naomi to lean into me. To pat me on the knee. To flirt.

She doesn't. She just thinks about it. Then she says, "I'm fine."

And it's so clear she's not.

"You lie," I tell her.

"Fine," she says again.

"Not fine."

"Fine."

I shake my head.

"Why do you lie?" I ask her.

"To cock-block truth."

Fair enough.

Naomi goes on. "Where did we get it in our heads that we need truth all the time? Sometimes lies are nice, you know? You don't have to know the truth all the time. It's too exhausting."

"These are all truths, Naomi."

She smiles. "I know."

"The No Kiss List," I say.

"The No Kiss List is dead." Naomi doesn't seem sorry to see it go.

"Yeah. But we should've put ourselves on it."

"I liked that lie."

"So did I."

"But not now."

"No, not now."

We are in such uncharted territory here. We had it all planned out, and in the past few weeks we've just taken an eraser to all of it. Our two different versions, which we hadn't realized were different. The maps are gone. The fantasies are gone. A little bit of the trust is gone. But even if we've erased all the lines and trajectories . . . even if we've blotted out all the hints and intimations . . . the writing on the map is gone, but the paper's still there. We are still here. You can't just erase hope and love and history. At the very least, you'd have to burn it. And if we're still here, we haven't burned.

"Shit, Naomi," I say.

"You're such a fuckhead," Naomi says.

And that's when she leans into me. When the top of her hair tilts into my cheek. When her head rests against my shoulder. When her hand finds my hand, and we hold.

"Bruce, huh?" she says after a moment's silence.

"Yeah," I tell her. "Bruce."

"You screwed it up?"

"Maybe?"

"Well, unscrew it. It would really suck if we went through all this over nothing."

I nod.

Naomi goes on. "I think I might have screwed it up with Gabriel, too. He kinda likes me. At least, I think he does. And I might want to try to like him back, only it's weird, and the timing is bad, and I really don't know what to do about it.

Gabriel made this mix for me. I think I was supposed to take all this hidden meaning from it, but I have no fucking clue. Then I made him a mix back. It sucked."

"Gabriel the doorman?" I ask.

"Jesus," Naomi says, hitting me with the hand I'm not holding, "where have you been?"

I suppose this isn't the time to tell her I've always thought Gabriel had big ears. Not freakishly big, but noticeable. Nice abs, though.

"So how can I help?" I ask.

"Do I even have to say it?"

"What?"

"God, we've got to get our wavelengths back in check. I need you to make a mix for me. I mean, a mix for him. Take his. Listen to it. Decipher. Then respond in kind. I'm too messed up right now to do it."

"You want me to Cyrano hot Gabriel for you?" I ask her.

"Yup. You can make penance that way. Meanwhile, I can continue on my crash course with academic oblivion."

"Meaning?"

"Meaning I'm failing Freshman Seminar and Comp Lit, thanks to stupendous lack of interest and effort. I fail those, I fail out of NYU."

Zoinks. Naomi has a big fucking problem here—much bigger than I realized.

"I'll help you. Let me write your papers."

She lets go of my hand and places hers on my leg. Then she turns to look at me—just *looks* at me. "No, Ely. Maybe that worked in high school, but no more. Truth is, failing out of NYU will be the last incentive Mom needs. She won't have to keep a job she hates so I can go to school there. That dream can die, too. Me going to college, and us clinging to the idea of Dad—those were the last lies we've had to live out. Maybe now we can move on. And move out."

"You can't move," I say. I mean, she *can't*.

"We'll see," she replies. But I can hear it in her voice: It's going to happen.

"Don't move too far," I manage to say.

I'm petrified by the idea of her moving away. Even when we were fighting, even when things were bad, I took some grounding from the fact that she was here. The idea of her leaving completely makes me feel like the ground's no longer there.

I guess she hears the desperation in my voice. The need.

"Oh, Ely," she says, leaning closer.

"Oh, Naomi," I say.

Is that all we need? Can the way we say each other's names encompass all our history, all our love, all our fear, all our fights, all our reunions, all of what we know about each other, all of what we don't know? Can that all be heard in the way she says "Ely" and the way I say "Naomi"?

I'm really not sure. But it's what we have.

We start talking. About her mom. About Bruce. About Gabriel. About the Robins and Bruce the First. About the possible benefits of transferring to Hunter College.

"Are we okay?" I finally ask.

She looks at me, and for a second I'm afraid she's going to say no. But instead she says, "Yeah, we're okay. Everything's changed, and you have to be ready to deal with that. But we're okay."

I can accept that. Just like I've accepted the fact that we're never going to be married, I'll have to accept the fact that she doesn't believe it anymore, either. We're where we need to be. It might not be as fun as it was before. But it's necessary.

She kisses me on the cheek.

"Go get Bruce. Bring 'im back alive."

I tell her I will . . . and then I'll return to make her a kick-ass mix for Gabriel.

"No," she says. "I changed my mind. I think there's another way."

I know better than to ask her for details. I take comfort in the fact that I'll know them soon enough.

She gets up and I get up. As she starts to head back upstairs, I say to her, "Wait . . . weren't you heading downstairs for a reason?"

She looks at me like I'm completely stupid.

"No," she says. "I knew you'd be here waiting."

And with that, she turns her corner, and I turn mine.

CLOSETS

I'm not drunk or stoned.

I may be crazy.

I don't care.

I find him in the supply closet.

Yes, doormen have supply closets. These closets, strangely, do not contain spare doors or spare doorknobs or even spare men (as far as I can tell). That's okay. I don't need a door or a doorknob. I only need one certain doorman.

Gabriel looks at me like I'm jailbait, like he already knows why I've decided to intrude on the doorman's one sanctuary, where they go to sneak smokes or to escape the Building residents during their fifteen-minute breaks or simply to find a spare lightbulb.

He's sitting at the workbench, wearing large headphones that still can't obscure his big ears. When he sees me, he glances at the clock on the wall, then turns off the music player and removes the headphones. "It's two in the morning, Naomi. What are you doing here?"

He knows the answer.

I take my stand under the lightbulb hanging from the ceiling.

Finally Gabriel says, "I could get fired for this."

"Don't worry about it," I tell him. "I'm bound by the co-op board's hatred of my family to tell you they'll blame me, not you."

He stands up, takes a step closer to me. "I'm bound by my own personal will to tell you I can't *not* be this building's doorman soon enough." Even under the harsh light that exposes all facial blemishes (his dark skin reveals none), he's so gorgeous my knees almost buckle from his nearness. But he doesn't reach for me, though he's close enough—he could. Perhaps he's noticing the blackheads on my nose?

So what about the imperfections.

I tug the string hanging from the lightbulb over his head. Lights out. I close my eyes, angle my head, ready to make this happen.

But the light is back on. I open one eye to see: Gabriel is not in about-to-kiss-Naomi pose. His head is tilted, yes, but his confused expression seems to ask, *What the* hell *is Naomi doing?*

WHAT DO I HAVE TO DO TO GET A KISS OUT OF A BOY I LIKE, ANYWAY?

"The doorman code of conduct?" I ask Gabriel. What did I do wrong this time? Or is Gabriel one of those Madonna/whore guys who can't deal with a girl who makes the first move?

"No, the gentleman's code of conduct," he says. "And, I

don't know, maybe needing better ambience? Like, not in a closet. Maybe dinner and a movie first?"

I really don't know how to do this. When the stakes count. I am an idiot.

I turn around to leave, embarrassed, but he presses his hand against the door to keep it from opening. (He really is a bad doorman.) Then he places the softest, sweetest kiss ever on the back of my neck. "We'll get there," he whispers in my ear.

🎵 *I got my kiss, I got my k-i-s-s.* 🎵

We leave the supply closet to head back into the lobby. His pinkie finger intertwines into mine.

Awesome, as girl-Robin might say.

"Ely left something for you at the front desk." Gabriel hands me a postcard of Buenos Aires, addressed to both me and Ely.

What I really wanted was an uno, dos, tres–*threesome with both of you. Love and happiness, Donnie Weisberg.*

I snort.

Damn. I really wish I wouldn't do that in front of the guy I like.

But Gabriel must truly like me, because he ignores my near-snarf. He says, "Ely came down here, dressed all spiffy like he was going somewhere important, asked me to give you this like he knew I'd be seeing you tonight, and walked out like he was on a mission. Then he came right back through the door fifteen minutes later and hasn't been back down since."

Ely chickened out.

I am not having this. I took my stand. He was supposed to take his. That's how we work.

I'm about to offer up an explanation for my sudden departure, but Gabriel just smiles at me. "Go," he says, looking toward the elevator and pointing ⋂.

My key to Ely's apartment is back under the doormat. I find him lying in his bed, staring at the ceiling.

A shiver runs through me, being back in Ely's bedroom. It's the same room as always, we weren't apart that long, but still—it feels different. The expectation of what could happen here is gone.

The time will come soon enough when I arrive home, expecting to see Ely, but he will not be there, because Mom and I will no longer be here. It's hard enough to imagine that Mom and I will eventually call some other building in this city our home; it's harder to imagine a home could exist for me in a place removed from Ely; the hardest part is recognizing that the distance *should* happen. ☺

I take Ely's leather coat from his closet and put it on. I'm cold. And so not dumpy.

"He was totally in here the night we had that fight, wasn't he?"

"Who? Where?" Ely mumbles. He looks comatose. Fearful. This isn't an Ely I know. He's a warrior. Isn't he?

"Bruce the Second. In the closet."

At the same time, Ely and I both exclaim: "With a candlestick!"

I pull the covers off him. "You're getting your best suit all crinkly, lying around like that."

"I ironed it," Ely says. "Can you believe that?"

"Well, it must be true love, then, Ely. And you look beautiful in that suit."

The timetable on the hurt is this: It still hurts. But less so. I can live with it. One day it may be gone.

He doesn't say anything.

I try again. "Are you scared of being hurt?"

He thinks about it. Then: "No. I'm scared of hurting him. Like I hurt you."

Somehow it's a relief to hear him say this, for him to acknowledge the difference in our feelings for one another, even if we can't seem to talk about that difference. I don't know that I could if I wanted to, anyway. The space filling the hurt and disappointment is still too big.

The wall was always there; we just chose to ignore it. Mostly, *I* chose to ignore it.

"Get up, Ely," I say. My new mantra. I might be a faith healer in my next life. For now, I'll probably settle for taking a time-out on the school thing and just get a job at Starbucks until Mom and I have figured out our next move. I'm thinking I will look great in that green apron. Maybe sometime in the near future, after many dinners and movies (hopefully he'll pay, because I'm a girl who can make the first move, but I am majorly broke), Gabriel will see me wearing . . . only that green apron?

Ely stands up. I want to smooth out the creases in his suit, but I don't. Instead I tell Ely about the secret spot where he can touch Bruce the Second, the place on his back that's so tender to him Bruce will profess his undying love whether he means it or not.

I'm sorry. I can make my peace with it. I don't think that means I have to like it.

"You're a bitch," Ely says. "But it's good advice."

I have a feeling Bruce the Second will mean it with Ely.

"I love you," I say. I mean it in the best possible way.

Usually I'd kiss him on the cheek at this point—perhaps with the expectation/hope of more. I don't now. I'll save that energy for the maybe of Gabriel. Or some guy who is at least → *straight* ←. "Now, go. Run to him."

The moms took us to see *Peter Pan* on Broadway when we were in second grade. I hated it. I wouldn't clap for Tinker Bell. That stupid fairy could die and I wouldn't care. But other parts, I got. I used to wish that if Ely and I ran fast enough, hard enough, together, the force of our energy could transform us, like Wendy and Peter Pan. Our legs would intertwine as they lifted us from the ground. We'd 🕊 away. Ely just had to want it as much as me.

"👁 ♥ U 2," he signs to me.

I almost tell Ely that Gabriel qualifies for the ~~No Kiss List~~™ as much as Bruce the Second does at this point, but I don't. I want to keep this one for myself, for now.

So I just say, "✌."

CLOSE

As I'm leaving the apartment, Naomi signs to me, "Don't worry, be happy."

I remember when we first decided to learn sign language—it was fourth grade, and we wanted to have our secrets even when our parents or our other friends were looking. Later on, it was great for clubs where the music was way too loud—we could still have a conversation without having to shout. Sometimes we'd bump into other people who knew ASL and we'd all talk to each other. But most of the time it was just me and Naomi, as always in our own two-person world.

I think about that as I head over to Bruce's, and I think that as hard as we try, it still sometimes feels like we all speak different languages. Even if we share all the same words, meanings can be different. And the mistake isn't in speaking the different languages, but in ignoring the fact. I thought Naomi and I had perfectly matched up our vocabularies and our definitions. But that's just not possible. There are always meanings that are different, words that are heard differently than they're said. There's no such thing as a soulmate . . . and who would want there to be? I don't want half of a shared soul. I want my own damn soul.

I think I'm going to learn to appreciate the word *close*. Because that's what Naomi and I are. We're close. Not all the way there. Not identical. Not soulmates. But close. Because that's as far as you should ever get with another person: very, very close.

That's what I want with Bruce, too.

I want to be close.

It's bullshit to think of friendship and romance as being different. They're not. They're just variations of the same love. Variations of the same desire to be close.

Robin and Robin come down to let me into the dorm— I want my first appearance to Bruce to be a knock on the door, not a buzz on the intercom.

Robin and Robin are in the middle of a fight over what Bill Murray whispers to Scarlett Johansson at the end of *Lost in Translation*—it's one of those total couple-fights where you can tell they're getting off on it even as they're slamming each other. It's fun to be in, I guess, but hell to be around.

I duck out and wind my way through the halls to Bruce's door. I'm so nervous I actually debate the proper way to knock. Friendly tap? Enthusiastic pound? Nursery-rhyme beat?

I go for the friendly tap. His "Who is it?" actually giddifies me further.

"It's me," I say. "Your long-lost boyfriend."

The door opens and Bruce takes in my suit, my anxious

smile. I take in . . . well, his I'm-not-going-out clothes. Stained green T-shirt, torn jeans.

Stop judging his clothes. Stop judging his clothes. Stop judging his clothes.

"Hi," he says, and from his voice I can tell I'm not the only nervous one here.

I guess I never got past the what-to-wear part of the planning stage, because I stand there like a statue of someone really stupid.

And that's when it turns into a musical. I mean, not literally. It's not like an orchestra starts playing or Bruce and I start singing. But I recognize this moment: It's the moment in the musical when the traveling salesman proclaims his love for the shy librarian. She doesn't believe it. He has to let her know. They're meant for each other—they both feel it—but only one of them believes it. It's time to take action, even if it's not easy. It's time to use the truth as a form of persuasion. I realize that.

As soon as I get into the room, as soon as the door closes, I'm singing the truth to him. The words are just coming out, and if there isn't any music, there's still a tune to what I'm saying. I'm telling him I've missed him. I'm telling him I don't understand what I did to make him disappear, but that whatever it was, I want to prevent it from happening again. I'm telling him that I know I'm not good enough for him, that I am this unreliable gay boy who always manages to mess up the things that mean the most to me. *This* is my language. *This* is how I can say what I need to say. This sudden musical number.

I don't say "I'm in love with you," because that's the sentence that's in every sentence, the feeling that's behind every word.

"I'm in love with you" comes out as "I know I'm a total flirty slut and I know that dating me is probably the kiss of death, and I'm sure if you polled my ex-boyfriends, eleven out of eleven of them would tell you to run screaming away from me. I know that I probably move too fast and I know that I get everything wrong all of the time and I know that you probably feel that you've come to your senses by deciding to get me out of your life. I know I am probably not worthy of how sweet you are and how nice you are and how smart you are. I know that I totally sprung myself on you and you've probably regretted it ever since. But I really, really hope that you feel that maybe there was something there, because I have a great time when I'm with you, and I feel like I could be the person I want to be when I'm with you, and I think I could treat you the way you deserve when I'm with you. And I realize that I'll probably fuck it all up, if I haven't fucked it up already, but I'm hoping that you might find it in your heart to maybe risk that and see what happens."

I stop then, and all the music is frozen in the air, waiting for the librarian's response. Either the notes are going to come to life again or they're going to fall to the ground and shatter like ice.

A pause. Then . . .

Bruce opens his mouth and sings back to me: "No—you

don't understand. *I'm* the one who's not good enough for *you.*"

And suddenly it's a duet.

"I'm not sexy," he sings.

"Yes, you are," I sing back.

"I'm too selfish," I sing.

"No, you're not," he sings back.

"I'm afraid," he sings.

"That's okay," I sing back.

"I'm afraid," I sing.

"That's okay," he sings back.

We always see our worst selves. Our most vulnerable selves. We need someone else to get close enough to tell us we're wrong. Someone we trust.

Yes, I know Bruce will never look good on the dance floor. I know he's got issues. I know he's a mutant.

But I like that.

I just have to convince him. The same way he needs to convince me he doesn't think I'm reckless and heartless.

This is what we need to do.

We know it won't all happen now. And it can't ever happen perfectly.

But we can get close.

He asks me why we haven't slept with each other yet, and I explain to him how I want to wait, how that means something, and I think of how stupid I've been not to explain it earlier, not to let him in on the meaning. And I ask him why he left the club that night, and he tells me how scared he was, how irrelevant he felt.

"I took you for granted," I say.

And he says, "No. I just bolted too soon. I should've said something to you. Then I would've known it was in *my* head, not yours."

I have been guilty before of kissing people to shut them up. I have kissed boys (and girls) out of pity or desire for power or just to be flirty. But when I kiss Bruce now—when we hold each other and kiss each other and try so hard to feel every ounce of it—I'm not trying to dodge anything or avoid anything or tease anything or control anything. It's love that kisses him. Pure and simple love.

If this were a musical, the orchestra would swoon to a stop, the audience would begin to applaud, the lights would go out. And then there'd be another number.

In this case, the librarian and the traveling salesman remain on the stage. They wait for the audience to file out of their seats. They wait for the orchestra to pack up its instruments and go home for the night. They stand there on the stage until it's just the two of them left.

Even with no one else around, they sing.

It's late when I get home to Naomi.

I pass Gabriel on the way to the elevator.

"You better be good to her" is all I say to him.

"I will be" is all he says back to me.

I tiptoe through my apartment, careful not to wake the

moms. I find Naomi sleeping in my bed—sleeping off all the sleeplessness of the past months, sleeping past all the tiredness. Seeing her like that, the sheets scrunched up in her hands (she's always been a total sheet-snatcher) and her one foot dangling over the side (she always likes it to be free), I feel like I know her. Really know her. And part of really knowing her is also knowing that I don't necessarily know her as well as I think I do. Which is okay. We should each have our own damn souls.

I take off my shoes, my jacket, my tie. She stirs a little when I climb onto the bed—on top of the sheets, careful. I have four pillows on my bed, each in an identical pillowcase, and yet she always knows the best one to take. I shift a little, make myself comfortable on the second-best pillow. I turn on my side so I can see her in the dark.

"How'd it go?" she asks me in a sleep-infused voice.

"Good," I say. "Really good."

"Thank God," she says, shifting her knee so that it touches mine. This is the closest we'll get all night—this is both the distance and the closeness that we need.

I could have stayed over with Bruce, but this is where I wanted to end my night. This is what I wanted to come back to. This is as much a part of my story as anything else. Friendship is love as much as any romance. And like any love, it's difficult and treacherous and confusing. But in the moment when your knees touch, there's nothing else you could ever want.

"Good night, Robin," I say.

"Good night, Robin," Naomi replies.

"Good night, Mrs. Loy."

"Good night, Kelly."

"Good night, Cutie Patootie."

"Cutie Pie."

"Sorry. Good night, Cutie Pie."

"Buenas noches, Donnie Weisberg."

"Good night, Dairy Queens."

"Good night, Bruce the First."

"Good night, Moms."

"Good night, Mom. And Dad."

"Good night, Gabriel the hot boyfriend."

"Good night, Bruce the good boyfriend."

"Good night, Naomi."

"Good night, Ely."

It's a total lie to say there's only one person you're going to be with for the rest of your life.

If you're lucky—and if you try really hard—there will always be more than one.

RACHEL COHN and DAVID LEVITHAN are writing together for the second time with *Naomi and Ely's No Kiss List*. Both are highly acclaimed young adult authors in their own right.

Rachel's previous books include *Gingerbread,* an ALA Best Book for Young Adults, an ALA Top Ten Quick Pick for Young Adults, and a *Publishers Weekly* and *School Library Journal* Best Book of the Year, as well as its sequels, *Shrimp,* a *Kirkus Reviews* Editors' Choice and a New York Public Library Book for the Teen Age, and *Cupcake.*

David's previous books include *Boy Meets Boy,* an ALA Top Ten Best Book for Young Adults, an ALA Quick Pick, and a Lambda Literary Award winner; *The Realm of Possibility,* an ALA Top Ten Best Book for Young Adults; *Are We There Yet?,* a New York Public Library Book for the Teen Age; and *Wide Awake.*

Rachel and David's first novel together, *Nick & Norah's Infinite Playlist,* is also available from Knopf.

Their Web sites are linked: www.rachelcohn.com and www.davidlevithan.com.